THE MYSTERIOUS PRESS

The Cellar

Also by Minette Walters

Minette Walters

The Cellar

The Mysterious Press
New York

First published in Great Britain by Arrow Books, part of the Penguin Random House group, in association with Hammer in 2015.

First Grove Atlantic hardcover edition: February 2016

First Grove Atlantic paperback edition: January 2017

Printed in the United States of America

ISBN 978-0-8021-2628-3
eISBN 978-0-8021-9025-3

The Mysterious Press
an imprint of Grove Atlantic
154 West 14th Street
New York, NY 10011

Distributed by Publishers Group West

groveatlantic.com

17 18 19 20   10 9 8 7 6 5 4 3 2 1

For Charlotte

'Passionate hatred can give meaning and purpose to an empty life.'

—Eric Hoffer

Darkness speaks.
It whispers words of comfort in the walls and
in the webs that spiders weave.
Darkness breathes.
Softly. Quietly.
Warming the air with its sweet-scented breath.
Darkness feels.
It coils its sinewy embrace about the thing it loves
and soothes away pain.
Darkness sees.
Darkness hears.

SUMMER

One

Muna's fortunes changed for the better on the day that Mr and Mrs Songoli's younger son failed to come home from school. Not immediately. Immediately, she felt great fear as Yetunde Songoli wailed and screamed and beat her with a rod because the ten-year-old wasn't in his room. It was Mr Songoli who put a stop to the punishment. Be sensible, he ordered his wife. The police will ask questions if they see bruises on her arms.

Shortly afterwards, Yetunde moved Muna to a room with a bed and a window. She pulled a brightly coloured dress over the girl's head and bound matching ribbons into her hair, hissing at her all the while for being a witch and a demon. Muna must have brought a curse on them. Why else had Abiola not come home?

Left alone, Muna stared at her reflection in the mirror on the wall. Was this what Mr Songoli had meant by being 'sensible'? To make Muna look pretty? It was very confusing. After a long time, she heard the sound of cars drawing up outside, the doorbell ringing and unknown voices speaking in the hall. She would have retreated to a darkened corner to squat on her haunches if Yetunde hadn't ordered her to sit on the bed. It was uncomfortable – her back began to hurt with the strain of staying upright – but she didn't move. Immobility had become a friend over the years. It allowed her to go unnoticed.

She was beginning to hope she'd been forgotten until she heard footsteps on the stairs. She recognised Yetunde Songoli's heavy tread but not the lighter one that followed behind. She stared impassively at the door, watching it open to reveal Yetunde's great, bloated body and a slim white woman, dressed in a shirt and trousers. Muna would have taken her for a man if her voice, when she spoke, hadn't been soft.

Yetunde lowered herself to the bed and put an affectionate arm around Muna's waist. She was so heavy that the mattress dipped beneath her weight and Muna could do nothing but lean against her. She was too small and thin to resist the woman's pull. Don't show fear, Yetunde warned in Hausa. Smile when this policewoman smiles at you, and speak in answer to the questions I ask you. It won't matter what you say. She's white English and doesn't understand Hausa.

Smile. Muna did her best to ape the soft curve of the white's lips but it was a long time since she'd done anything so unnatural. *Speak.* She opened her mouth and moved her tongue but nothing came out. She was too afraid to voice aloud what she practised in whispers to herself each night. Yetunde would know for certain she had demons if she said something in English.

'How old is she?' the white asked.

Yetunde stroked Muna's hand. 'Fourteen. She's my first-born but her brain was damaged at birth and she finds it hard to learn.' Tears dripped down the bloated cheeks. 'Was this not tragedy enough? Must my precious Abiola be another?'

'There's no reason to think the worst yet, Mrs Songoli. It's not unusual for ten-year-old boys to truant from time to time. I expect he's at a friend's house.'

'He's never truanted before. The school should have called my husband at work when they didn't get me. We pay them enough. It's irresponsible to leave a message on an answerphone.'

The white crouched down to put herself on the same level as Muna. 'You say you've been out all day, but what about your daughter? Where was she?'

'Here. We have permission to teach her at home. A Hausa speaker comes to tutor her each morning.' Yetunde's bejewelled fingers moved from caressing Muna's hand to stroking her cheek. 'Children can be so cruel. My husband wouldn't want her teased for her disability.'

'Does she have any English?'

'None. She struggles even to speak Hausa.'

'Why didn't her tutor answer the phone when the school rang?'

'It's not her job. She wouldn't take a call intended for some-one else.' Yetunde pressed a tissue to her eyes. 'It's so rare for me to go out. Any other day I would have been here.'

'You said the first you knew that something was wrong was when you returned at six o'clock and listened to your messages.' The crouching white examined Muna's face. 'Yet it must have worried your daughter that Abiola didn't come home at his usual time. Will you ask her why she didn't tell you as soon as you opened the door?'

Yetunde pinched Muna's waist. She's talking about Abiola. Look at me and pretend concern. Say something.

Muna turned her head and whispered the only words she was permitted to use. Yes, Princess. No, Princess. Is there something I can do for you, Princess?

Yetunde dabbed at her eyes again. 'She says she thought he was with our older son, Olubayo. He takes his little brother to

5

the park sometimes.' A great sigh issued from her chest. 'I should have been here. So much time has been wasted.'

Muna wondered if the white would believe such a lie, and kept her gaze lowered for fear the blue eyes would read in hers that Yetunde was being deceitful. Muna's life was less painful for being thought too simple to learn any language but Hausa.

'You realise we need to search the house and garden, Mrs Songoli?' said the white, rising to her feet. 'It's standard procedure when a child goes missing. Abiola may have hidden himself away rather than go to school. We'll make it as easy on you as we can but I suggest you take your daughter downstairs so that your family can sit together in one room.'

If Muna had known how to see humour in a situation, she might have laughed to hear Yetunde order Olubayo to treat her as his sister. But humour and laughter were as alien to her as smiling and speaking. Instead she thought of the kicks and slaps Olubayo would give her once the whites had left. He was big for a thirteen-year-old, and Muna feared for herself when he changed from boy to man. So many times recently she'd looked up from her work to find him staring at her and rubbing his groin against the door frame.

From beneath lowered lids, she watched the expressions on Mr and Mrs Songoli's faces. How anxious they were, she thought, but was it Abiola's disappearance that was worrying them or having police in their house? As Yetunde had brought her downstairs, Muna had seen that the door to the cellar was open. A bulb now glowed in the overhead light at the top of the steps, banishing the darkness she'd lived in and showing her that her mattress and small bag of possessions had been removed from the stone floor at the bottom.

She thought how harmless her prison looked, brightly lit and with nothing to show that anyone had slept there, and it gave her a small hope that whites were kinder than blacks. Why would the Songolis hide the truth about her otherwise? Just once, Muna shifted her glance fractionally to look at the woman in trousers. She was asking Olubayo about Abiola's friends, and Muna felt a shock of fear to find the blue eyes staring at her and not at the boy. They seemed clever and wise and Muna trembled to think this person knew she understood what was being said.

Would she guess that Muna had listened to the message being left on the answerphone and had known all day that Abiola had not arrived at his school?

The searchers returned, shaking their heads and saying there was no sign of the child although they'd found a mobile telephone on charge in his room. Yetunde identified it as Abiola's and began to wail again because her son hadn't had it with him. She rocked to and fro issuing high ululations from her mouth, while her husband strode angrily about the carpet, cursing the day he'd brought his family to this godforsaken country. He bunched his fists and thrust his blood-infused face into the white woman's, demanding to know what the police were doing.

Muna would have cowered before such ferocity, but not the white. She took Ebuka calmly by the arm and returned him to his chair to weep for his beloved son. She seemed to have great power over men. Where Yetunde stamped and raged to get what she wanted, the white gave quiet orders that were obeyed. She used the telephone to request a child-protection officer to examine Abiola's computer and smartphone. She asked Yetunde and Ebuka for photographs and videos of the boy. Bags containing his clothes, toothbrush and comb were taken away. Sandwiches and pizzas were brought in.

All the while she asked questions of the family. Had Abiola been unhappy recently? Was he bullied? Did he shut himself in his room, spending long hours on the internet? Was he a boy of secrets? How much did his parents know about his friends? Did he run with a gang? Was he taken to school each morning or did he make his own way? Who had seen him off that morning?

The picture Yetunde and Ebuka painted in their answers was not one that Muna recognised. They described Abiola as a popular boy who walked to class with his brother each morning, keen to begin his lessons. They made no mention that he wet his bed most nights and slapped and kicked his mother if she asked him to do something he didn't like. He had to be bribed with sugary foods to go to school, fed to him in titbits from Yetunde's fingers. It was why mother and son were as fat and bloated as each other. For every sticky sweet Yetunde gave Abiola, she took one herself.

This trouble had come upon them, Muna thought, because Mr Songoli had cancelled the car that had driven the boys to class each morning and brought them back each afternoon. He was angered at how spoilt they'd become and told them they must learn to want their education as strongly as the bush children in Africa. Now Olubayo told terrible lies about the happenings that morning, swearing hand on heart that he had walked Abiola to the school gates. Yet Muna knew this couldn't be true. Olubayo had so much hatred for Abiola, and Abiola so much hatred for him, that they never did anything together.

Perhaps the white didn't believe the story either for she asked Yetunde if she'd seen the boys leave. And of course Yetunde said she had. She would never admit to her husband that she'd been sitting before her mirror, massaging expensive bleaching cream into her skin. Such wasteful extravagance annoyed Ebuka.

'I'd like to ask your daughter the same question, Mrs Songoli. Will you put it to her?'

Yetunde raised her voice. Look up, Muna. This woman is asking if you saw Olubayo and Abiola leave this morning. Nod your head and say something. She expects you to speak.

Muna did as she was asked. Yes, Princess. No, Princess. Is there something I can do for you, Princess? But even as she whispered in Hausa she longed for the courage to say the words she practised to herself each night.

'Please help me. My name is Muna. Mr and Mrs Songoli stole me when I was eight years old. I would like to go home but I don't know who my parents are or where I come from.'

Two

The only adults Muna could recall from her childhood were nuns and priests with shiny white skin. The years had blurred their features and muddled their names but she thought she'd been happy during the time she spent with them. She found it easier to remember the beaming black faces of the children. There was more to recognise in people she resembled. She dreamed sometimes of playing games in the dust of a sun-drenched schoolyard, full of colour and brightness, but where that was and why she had been there, she didn't know.

The life she lived now had begun the day Yetunde came to claim her. The woman, tall and magnificently dressed in a bright blue kaba with a matching gele on her head and gold necklaces around her neck, had documents to prove her entitlement to the child. With a happy laugh, she had claimed Muna as her niece, hugging and kissing her and telling her how pretty she was, and Muna had smiled into the woman's eyes as if she knew her. No priest would question the love he saw between them, particularly when Yetunde Songoli produced a legal writ giving her guardianship of her dead sister's eight-year-old daughter.

Had Muna been suspicious? No. Her only feeling had been awe to discover she belonged to someone as rich and beautiful as Aunt Yetunde. If an explanation had been offered for why she had ever been placed in the care of nuns or why Yetunde Songoli had thought to look for her there, she didn't remember. Her strongest recollection of the day was skipping through the schoolyard gates at her aunt's side without a backward glance at the place she'd called home.

Now, all these years later – *five, six, seven?* – Muna wished her memories of it were stronger. Reason told her it must have been an orphanage and that her surname, if she'd ever had one, wasn't known to the priest. Or perhaps he was as wicked as Yetunde Songoli? Perhaps he posed as a priest to make money from selling motherless girls to well-dressed women with documents? Muna didn't want to believe that. She longed to think white people had more kindness than black ones, but in her heart she knew it wasn't true. She had seen the cold and unfriendly way they passed each other in the street outside this house where she lived, not caring to exchange a greeting or even smile.

Her worst terrors came during the night. She could believe in herself in daylight, but alone in the pitch-blackness of the cellar she doubted her very existence. However hard she strained to see the walls and the floor, even her hand before her face, there was only darkness. And the darkness was more alive than she was.

Only pain told her she was real. When she touched the scars between her thighs where part of her had been cut away by a witch, her eyes shed tears of anguish. It will make you pure, the woman had said as Yetunde held her down and the knife sliced through those parts that were private to little Muna.

The word meant nothing to Muna for she couldn't see that the agony she suffered each time Ebuka ripped new tears in her misshapen hole made her pure. She didn't know why he did it and shook with dread each time the cellar door opened and his torch shone down the steps. She never saw his face. He became as invisible as she was once the light was quenched and he clamped his hand across her mouth to stifle her whimpers. She could only tell it was Ebuka from his smell and his pig-like grunts.

Perhaps purity came from the searing pain of passing water or the fear she felt of the mysterious blood that had begun to leak from her once a month. Now Ebuka only visited her when she bled as if what leaked from him could be cleansed by what leaked from Muna.

Yetunde asked her often if she had begun to bleed between her legs but she always said no. She felt it was a secret she should keep though she didn't know why. She had little knowledge of anything except cooking and cleaning, and she'd learned those skills through being beaten with a rod when she made a mistake. There was so much that was unexplained in her life. Who she was. Where she had come from. How old she was. What place she was in and how she had got there.

She remembered climbing into a silver car outside the schoolyard gates and being driven through streets teeming with people and markets, and she remembered Aunt Yetunde smiling as she popped a coconut sweet between her lips. After that, Muna's memories were confused and random. She could recall the witch with the knife because the pain had caused her to wake and cry out, but most of the time she thought she'd been asleep.

Certain images kept recurring in her mind. Yetunde pushing coconut sweets between her lips. The feel of a man's beard against her cheek as he carried her in his arms through a large hall. The sound of Yetunde saying the child was his daughter. The roar of engines. People sitting in rows. A sense of lifting from the ground. Being carried through another hall. Rain on her face. Waking here in the darkness of this cellar and never tasting coconut again.

Muna thought the bearded man must have been Ebuka, but she had no explanation for why he had once pretended to be her father. She guessed the other memories were about a journey. The place she had left had been full of sunshine and colour but the only brightness here was in the greenness of the grass and the leaves on the trees. She wished she had made a mark each time they turned to golden brown for it meant another year had passed, but her child's mind had been too intent on counting each hour of the day to think about the future.

Through the bedroom windows upstairs, she could see over the high brick wall that surrounded the house. Away in the distance were tall buildings that reached towards the sky, but close too were houses like this one, hidden behind walls and obscured by trees. She saw more through the metal gates at the end of the short driveway when she was dusting the downstairs rooms than she ever saw upstairs. People walking. People in cars. It's how she knew she was in a world of whites. She came to recognise those who passed the gates each day but they never glanced in Muna's direction.

If they had she'd have jumped behind the curtains out of fear. She wasn't allowed to raise her eyes to anyone. She whispered words at night to remind herself she had a voice, but her dread of being heard was terrible. Yetunde had said Muna had demons inside her when she begged to go back to the schoolyard she knew, and had poured burning oil on the child's bare foot to teach her that demons spoke words of ingratitude.

Are you not happy to serve your aunt? Yetunde had asked. Yes, Princess, Muna had answered.

Muna was very afraid the white in trousers could see through her skull and into her brain. She could feel the sharpness of the clever blue eyes boring into her head. Had her ears told her that Muna had used the same phrases twice? A knot of sickening fear tightened in Muna's belly. Yetunde would wield the rod with even more cruelty if she could blame little Muna for the police not believing her.

'Did you look to see if Abiola entered the gates after you?' the white asked Olubayo.

'No. I ran to join my own friends.' Olubayo gave a sudden wail as if he knew he should show grief.

'Do you blame my son for this?' Ebuka Songoli demanded angrily.

'Of course not, sir, but we'll require the names of everyone he remembers at the gates when he arrived. We have a team searching the school premises in case Abiola met with an accident, but if he never went in, a parent or child may have seen what happened to him.' She paused. 'We need to establish if he left on his own or in the company of someone else.'

'A stranger has taken him. This is a terrible country. Such things would never happen in ours.'

'It's more likely to be someone he knew, Mr Songoli. The area was too crowded and too well covered by CCTV for a stranger abduction. One of my team is going through this morning's footage with the caretaker but any names Olubayo can give me will help. Tomorrow's Friday. It gives us little time to find witnesses before the students leave for the weekend.'

Muna sensed Olubayo's nervousness on the seat beside her as he stammered out those he remembered. She thought him foolish to do it. Did he think no one would have noticed that he arrived alone? On each of the four days since the car had been cancelled, he had taken to his heels as soon as he and Abiola were hidden from Yetunde's view by the wall surrounding the garden. Muna, whose first job every morning was to tidy the boys' attic bedrooms, had watched it happen. While Olubayo ran away laughing, his fat brother waddled and wept in a furious rage behind him.

It hadn't occurred to her to speak of it to Yetunde for Olubayo would have kicked her and slapped her if she had. Nor did she want to be beaten with the rod for pausing in her duties to tell Princess things she didn't want to hear. Muna's task was to wash Abiola's sheets, not care if he was abandoned in the road. She had no liking for him. He was a lazy, dirty boy who soiled his bed because Muna was there to clean it for him. Sometimes he smeared faeces on the linen to make the task of bleaching it harder.

Laziness had made him stupid and for that Muna could thank him. He had found it so hard to learn English that Mr Songoli had paid for him to be taught in the house. Since Yetunde wasn't interested in listening, the lessons had taken place in the dining room; and since Muna wasn't allowed to be seen by strangers, she was ordered to stay in the kitchen while the teacher was there. She had often wondered why Yetunde hadn't realised she would be able to hear what was said through the hatchway that linked the two rooms.

Perhaps Yetunde believed what she always said, that Muna was too feeble-minded to make her own way in the world. Be grateful for my protection, she would say as she struck with the rod whenever Muna displeased her. Without a place in the Songoli home, you would be nothing.

Muna was forbidden to watch television or listen to a radio, but even squatting in her place in the corner of the kitchen, she could hear what the family heard because they turned the volume so high. At first, she had only understood the language of Olubayo and Abiola's children's programmes, but as the years passed she absorbed the vocabulary of the daytime chat shows that Yetunde loved. And when Ebuka came home in the evening, she listened to the language of current affairs as she prepared the evening meals.

War . . . murder . . . rape . . . violence . . . hatred . . . intolerance . . . cruelty . . .

Muna could speak whole sentences in her head but she struggled to make her mouth say them. And more often than not she wondered if it was worth trying. From everything she heard, the world outside was as terrible and frightening as Yetunde and Ebuka Songoli described it.

Three

A week passed. Abiola's face kept appearing on television, and Mr Songoli raged about journalists and cameramen camped at his gate, pointing their lenses at his windows. The fingerprints of everyone in the house were taken, while others were lifted from the furniture in Abiola's bedroom. Olubayo was exposed as a liar when the CCTV footage showed that he arrived at school alone, and, worse, that Abiola never arrived at all. A woman in a neighbouring street said she'd seen a black boy being lifted into a car of the same make and colour as Mr Songoli's.

The house was searched a second time, far more thoroughly, and Ebuka and Yetunde were taken away for several hours to be questioned elsewhere. While they were gone, the white brought a Hausa speaker to question Muna. She was a woman of Yetunde's age who spoke impatiently and stared hard at the girl as she translated the white's words, adding phrases of her own.

This officer's name is Inspector Jordan, she said. Look up when you speak to her. Answer freely. You've no need to be nervous. There's nothing to fear if you tell the truth.

Muna doubted that. She had seen how viciously Ebuka had beaten Olubayo for bringing dishonour on the family with his lies. What if this Hausa speaker was a friend of Yetunde's and refused to repeat what Muna said about the Songolis stealing her from an orphanage? The white – Inspector Jordan – would learn nothing and this woman would tell Yetunde of Muna's ingratitude afterwards. And Muna dreaded to think of the punishment she would receive.

Life was better as the Songolis' disabled daughter. With a police liaison officer in the house, Muna no longer had to clean and cook from morning to night, sleep in the dark cellar or dress in a servant's clothes. Instead she was allowed to wear the same sort of pretty dresses that Yetunde wore, go to bed in a room with windows and electric light and sit with the family each evening, watching and listening as the search for Abiola continued.

Some of Inspector Jordan's questions were easy, needing simple yes or no answers. Do you love Abiola? *Yes.* Did you see him leave for school that morning? *Yes.* Did he come back after Olubayo abandoned him? *No.* Do you think Olubayo would have harmed his brother? *No.* Do you think your father might have harmed him? *No.*

Some were harder because Yetunde had told such ill-considered lies at the start. What is the name of the woman who comes to teach you each day? *There is no woman.* Why did your mother say there was? *She was afraid.* Of what? *That you'd make me go to school.* Don't you want to learn? *My parents teach me. They are kind about my slowness.* Wouldn't you rather go to class as your brothers do? *Not if I'm teased.*

The most dangerous questions concerned what Muna had been doing on the day that Abiola disappeared. Had she stayed in the house after Mrs Songoli left to meet her friend? What did she do to occupy her time? Muna told the truth. *I cleaned and tidied for Mamma.* Why didn't you notice that Abiola hadn't come home at his usual time? *I can't tell the time.* Weren't you worried when Olubayo came back alone? *I didn't know he was alone.* Why not? *I didn't see him. I was in Mamma's room, trying on her gold necklaces.*

The conversation seemed interminable, but when it ended the translator turned to Inspector Jordan and said she didn't believe Muna was lying. 'She's too unsophisticated to fabricate stories. She has trouble speaking at all so I imagine it was the left side of her brain that was damaged. The words she uses are very simple but her mouth finds even those hard to form.'

'But she sits so still and shows so little expression. Every instinct I have says something's wrong. She's small for four-teen . . . and her skin's a lot paler than her parents'. She doesn't smile . . . doesn't frown . . . barely reacts to anything, in fact.'

'I doubt she goes out much. You'll have to ask her mother. It may be that the motor function in the muscles of her face are impaired.'

'Her eyes work well enough. Why won't she look at me?'

'She leads a closeted life. Strangers frighten her.' The Hausa speaker studied Muna's bent head. 'She comes from a different culture. You may not be reading her correctly.'

'Except I had the strong impression she was afraid of her mother that first night. I'm certain she knows more than she's telling us.'

'Do you really think Mr and Mrs Songoli are involved in their son's disappearance?'

'It depends if Abiola ever left the house that morning. There are several witnesses who remember seeing Olubayo in the road but none who remember his brother.'

'What about the woman who saw a black boy being put in a car?'

'The description she gave doesn't match Abiola's.'

'Whites are notoriously bad at describing blacks. Most of you can't even differentiate between shades of brown.'

A smile entered the Inspector's voice. 'Maybe so, but it's hard to confuse a slender boy with a ten-year-old so grossly over-weight that he had to walk with his legs apart. According to the school, he weighed in excess of eleven stone. It's hard to imagine anyone lifting him . . . let alone a predatory paedophile looking for an easy target.'

'A dead weight's even heavier. If he died in this house, who carried him to the car? It would have needed both parents, wouldn't it?'

'And both to pull him out at the other end when they found a place to hide the body,' the white agreed. 'If one's involved, it's almost certain the other is as well.'

Muna would have feared for herself if Inspector Jordan and the Hausa speaker hadn't been in the house when Mr and Mrs Son-goli returned. Ebuka's anger was terrible to behold, and he would have taken it out on her if he hadn't had to pretend she was his daughter. He accused the police of being racists for putting him and his wife through the indignity of an interrogation, and raged at Scotland Yard for appointing a woman to run the investigation.

How dare such an insignificant person suggest that he or Yetunde had had anything to do with Abiola's disappearance? A woman's job was to run her kitchen, not exercise authority in a police force.

The translator took him to task in Hausa. In this country it was an offence to make sexist remarks, she warned sternly, and Mr Songoli showed his ignorance by doing so. As father to Abiola, he would have been interviewed in the same way whatever his colour for it was a sad – but true – statistic that children were more in danger inside their own homes than on the street.

Ebuka ignored her. 'Abiola was loved and treasured by his family,' he roared at the Inspector. 'My mistake was to cancel the taxi that took him to school. My son was taken because he was walking. Are you too foolish to understand that?'

'We have only Olubayo's word that he ever reached the end of the road, Mr Songoli. Despite numerous pleas for witnesses, no one has come forward to say they saw Abiola.'

'And because of that you accuse us? Why? You've searched our house from top to bottom and brought dogs into our garden . . . and you've found nothing. Have you done the same with the other properties in this road?'

Inspector Jordan nodded. 'All your neighbours gave my team permission to enter.'

'And have you found Abiola?'

'No.'

Ebuka jabbed a finger at her chest. 'Then I'm proved right,' he declared. 'My child was taken by a stranger on his way to school.'

Muna watched the Inspector take a step backwards. 'We think it more likely Abiola stayed here, Mr Songoli. His teachers say he was a reluctant student, and they all agree he would have chosen a day at home over one in class, particularly as he knew his mother would be out.'

Ebuka glared at her angrily before turning on Yetunde with a raised fist. Does she speak the truth? he demanded in Hausa. You said you were in this house for an hour after the boys left. Were you lying? Did you see him return?

Yetunde flinched. Of course not, my husband. Would I stay silent over something so important?

Inspector Jordan caught Ebuka's wrist and forced his arm to his side. 'You have a bad temper, sir. I suggest you bring it under control before you give your wife even more cause for anxiety.' She turned to the Hausa speaker. 'What did he say? Why was he threatening her?'

The woman's translation was precise.

The Inspector nodded. 'This is what we know, Mr Songoli. Your son hid in the summer house at some point. It may have been Wednesday evening or Thursday morning. We found sweet wrappers and empty crisp packets on the floor with his fingerprints on them. Your contract gardener swears they weren't there on Wednesday afternoon . . . and we have no reason to disbelieve him since I understand Mrs Songoli is very particular about litter.'

'But the gardener's not a man to be trusted,' wailed Yetunde. 'I have to watch him all the time to make sure he does as he's told. Who's to say he didn't take my child?'

'You and the elderly couple who employ him on Thursdays. You say Abiola left this house at eight fifteen last Thursday morning – the day he went missing – and the couple say the gardener was with them, some *twelve* miles away, from seven thirty until four in the afternoon.'

There was a long pause before Ebuka sank into a chair with a groan, clapping his hands to his head as if he were in pain. 'Is this why I've been interviewed so harshly today? And why my car has been impounded? Do you think Abiola was here when I came home from work that day? Do you think I lost my temper with him when I learned he'd been truanting?'

'You waited a long time to contact us, Mr Songoli. Your wife says she phoned you at your office at six when she came home and discovered Abiola wasn't here . . . yet your emergency call to us wasn't made until eight twenty-three. That's almost two and a half hours unaccounted for.'

Muna listened to Ebuka huff and puff about being caught in traffic and taking time to search the house himself, claiming it would have been foolish to summon the police if Abiola had been hiding under a bed. He made no mention of clearing the cellar of Muna's mattress and possessions or having to wait while Yetunde unpacked trunks of her old clothes, looking for a kaba small enough to fit the girl. Even then the yellow garment had been too big, and the woman had hissed with fury at having to sacrifice one of her scarves to create a sash about Muna's waist. All these things had taken time.

Inspector Jordan stayed silent until Ebuka drew breath. 'Are you saying you knew before you called us that Olubayo hadn't taken Abiola to school?' she asked.

Ebuka looked confused. 'I don't understand.'

'Why bother to look under beds if you believed what Olubayo told you? The first thing you said to us was that a stranger must have abducted your son – and you've continued to repeat that accusation all week – yet now you want me to believe you wasted over two hours looking for Abiola here. Why, Mr Songoli?'

Ebuka didn't answer.

'You'd do better to tell us the truth, sir.'

Ebuka looked to his wife for help, and Yetunde pointed a trembling finger at Muna. 'This girl can tell you if Abiola was here when Ebuka came back.'

'She says he wasn't.'

'Then why do you doubt my husband?'

The Inspector glanced at Muna's bent head. 'Your daughter's word isn't good enough, Mrs Songoli. We need provable facts, not hesitant responses from a child with learning difficulties. At the moment, we don't even know if Abiola was alive on Thursday morning. The last sighting of him by anyone other than this family was at three thirty the previous afternoon, the *Wednesday* . . . some twenty-nine hours before your husband reported him missing.'

Four

Muna thought Ebuka very foolish to lose his temper again. Perhaps he felt free to do it because the Hausa speaker had left, but he should have learned by now that the white was cleverer than he was. While he shouted angrily that his word could be believed, Inspector Jordan took some papers from a case on the table and showed them to him. She said they were copies of the witness statements he and his wife had signed after their interviews at the police station.

'The highlighted paragraphs show where your stories differ. You couldn't even agree on the events of Wednesday evening, Mr Songoli. You described prayers, followed by a formal family dinner and bedtime at eight o'clock. Mrs Songoli said Olubayo and Abiola ate supper in front of the television before going upstairs when their father came home. Which is true?'

Yetunde answered. 'My husband confused Wednesday with Tuesday. The explanation I gave is the correct one.'

Inspector Jordan selected another paper from her case. 'My team is studying footage from every CCTV camera in the roads around this house, your sons' school and Mr Songoli's office. This is a photograph of Abiola crossing the High Street at three thirteen on Wednesday afternoon. Shortly afterwards one of your neighbours claims to have seen him turn into your gate. She says it was around three thirty which supports the time stamp on this still.'

Yetunde bridled. 'Isn't that what I told the interviewer?' she demanded. 'Did you think I was lying?'

'I'm simply demonstrating how easy it is for us to prove or disprove what people tell us, Mrs Songoli. For example, you said your sons went to their bedrooms when their father came home . . . but that isn't true. We have Mr Songoli's car on camera, passing the traffic lights two streets down at six thirty-seven that Wednesday evening, and Olubayo's computer showing unbroken usage from five until just before midnight. I can even tell you what he was looking at.'

Olubayo was sitting next to Muna on the sofa, and she felt a shiver of alarm run through his body. It pleased her to have the police know he was a dirty boy as well as a liar. Muna had seen what he was watching when Yetunde ordered her to take a tray of food to his room – naked white ladies in strange positions – and, though she'd averted her gaze from Olubayo as she put the tray on the bed, she'd heard his animal grunts as he worked on himself. It had made her afraid that it wouldn't be long before he tried to leak his filth into her the way his father did.

'Abiola's computer wasn't used at all that day,' the white continued, 'yet his normal practice was to switch on at around four o'clock. Both boys' hard drives show a habit of doing a half to one hour's homework each night but neither followed that pattern on Wednesday. Do you have an explanation for that? Perhaps Olubayo can tell me.'

Ebuka spoke to his son in Hausa. *Say nothing, boy. I will do the speaking for all of us.* 'Why do you take no account of our distress at the loss of our son?' he demanded. 'If my wife and I are confused about that evening, it's because we haven't slept since Abiola was taken from us. How can we remember details from a week ago when our hearts and minds are broken with grief?'

'Most parents do, Mr Songoli. They agonise over everything said and done in the hours before a son or daughter goes missing. Even when they know the fault's not theirs, they still feel guilt for what's happened.'

'I've already admitted my mistake in cancelling the car.'

The Inspector nodded before holding up two more photographs. 'This is yours passing through the Crendell Avenue junction at six thirty-seven on Wednesday evening, and this' – she held up the second – 'is the same car driving through it in the opposite direction four and a half hours later. The time stamp says eleven seventeen. I believe you're the only driver in the house, sir. Do you want to tell me where you were going so late on the night before you say Abiola vanished?'

From beneath lowered lids, Muna saw fear in Ebuka's face and shock in Yetunde's. Neither answered.

'Mrs Songoli said she went to bed early and was asleep by ten thirty. You agreed with her – it's one of the few details that isn't in dispute – but you claimed you followed shortly afterwards and were in bed by eleven. And that's not true, is it, sir? Where did you go? We'll examine the footage from every camera within a ten-mile radius if we have to.'

It was Yetunde who spoke. You mustn't answer, she whispered in Hausa. This white has set a trap for you but she can't do anything if you refuse to speak. Phone your employer and ask him to send a solicitor.

Ebuka, paler than Muna had ever seen him, nodded. He left the room to make some calls and an hour later a man came to the house. He gave his name as Jeremy Broadstone and showed no fear of the Inspector when he accused her of trampling on his clients' rights. He ordered her and her colleagues from the room, and Muna was frightened by the power he had to make them leave when she heard the sound of tyres on the gravel outside. She feared the police had gone for good, and it caused her to dislike Jeremy Broadstone.

He was white and thin and beaky-nosed, and she thought him untrustworthy. He lowered himself into a chair without invitation and tapped his watch. 'We have limited time. I'm here because your employer, John Ndiko, asked me to come but I can't help you unless you're honest with me, Mr Songoli. Why do the police think you're involved in your son's disappearance? What cause have you given them for suspicion?'

Ebuka turned to his wife. 'This is not for their ears,' he said, nodding to Muna and Olubayo. 'Take them to their rooms while I speak to Mr Broadstone.'

But Yetunde refused. I will not, she answered in Hausa. If you've been visiting whores again, I want to know about it. You'll not keep secrets from me.

Will you shame me in front of this white?

You've brought shame on yourself through your own actions, she snapped. Don't blame me for how this man perceives you. She turned to Muna. Look up, girl, and smile as a daughter should. You and Olubayo are to go to your rooms. If there are any policemen in the hall, Olubayo will tell them the solicitor has asked to speak with us privately. Show your parents affection by giving each of us a kiss before you leave.

Muna watched Olubayo touch his mouth to Yetunde's cheek before rising to perform the task herself. It wasn't something she understood or had ever done. There was no pleasure in the sensation – the smell of Yetunde's skin repulsed her – but kissing Ebuka was worse. Perhaps he remembered how often he'd placed his hand across Muna's mouth in the darkness of the cellar because he wouldn't look at her when she lowered her face to his. The feel and smell of his rough beard was as unpleasant to her as always.

She felt a small relief as she closed the door behind her for it seemed the Songolis' honesty didn't stretch to admitting she wasn't their daughter, and her relief grew when she heard the sound of voices in the kitchen. The words were inaudible but she could tell from the lightness of tone that one belonged to Inspector Jordan and the other to the liaison officer. She raised her eyes to Olubayo, who was watching her from the foot of the stairs.

They won't be here for ever, Olubayo told her triumphantly. And then you'll be back where you belong. He tapped the panels of the cellar door. A filthy bitch in a filthy kennel.

Muna eyed him warily.

It makes me sick having to say I'm your brother. You're too stupid to be a Songoli. You don't understand anything.

The Devil whispered rebellion in Muna's ear. She took a step forward. 'My name is Muna,' she said in English. 'Mr and Mrs Songoli stole me when I was eight years old. I would like to go home.' She watched in satisfaction as Olubayo's eyes widened. The words had sounded right. She tried some others she'd practised. 'Mr Songoli beat Abiola with a rod. He fell to the floor and did not get up. I have not seen him since.'

Olubayo stared at her in shock, and Muna was thrilled at how easy it was to frighten him. She continued in Hausa.

If I say those words to the police, the Master will be taken away . . . and that will please me as much as it pleases me that Abiola is gone. He was a nasty boy and my life is better without him.

She watched tears ooze on to Olubayo's cheeks and despised him for it. Each day he had kicked his fat brother's legs and told him how much he hated him, and each evening he stamped his feet when Ebuka told him to do his homework. Another few steps brought her to the cellar door. Curiosity made her open it and touch the light switch. Once again she thought how benign it looked in the soft glow of the bulb. It had the appearance of a storage room. Boxes, trunks and cases were piled against the walls, and a table, covered in files from Ebuka's office, stood where her mattress had been.

She wondered what Ebuka had done with her bedding. From watching the police search the house the second time, Muna had seen how carefully they examined everything, and she knew they would have found it if it had been in the house. She guessed he'd used his car to take it away while Yetunde was dressing her in the spare room, and the idea gave her a warm feeling. The Inspector would show him another photograph soon.

She switched off the light and listened to the darkness. But if it was whispering to her she couldn't hear it above the murmur of voices coming from the kitchen. The Master will never send me back to the cellar, she told Olubayo, closing the door. He's afraid the white will find out about the bad things he's done. I see fear in his eyes each time he looks at her.

She turned with the same impassive face she always had, and watched the boy back away from her up the stairs. She enjoyed the power she felt when she saw how his hand trembled on the banister.

Some time later, Yetunde came to Muna's room and pleaded with her to help Ebuka. You must persuade the white that Abiola was alive on Thursday morning, she said. Mr Broadstone thinks she's more likely to believe you than Mr Songoli or myself.

How can I do that, Princess?

Describe what he was wearing and what he did . . . how he came to my room for sugared almonds . . . how he cried about having to walk to school.

But I didn't see him, Princess. I'm not allowed to look at any of you without permission. I waited in the kitchen until it was safe to go upstairs and take the sheets from Abiola's bed. It's what I do every day.

Then *pretend* you saw him, Yetunde snapped. You know he was here. His tantrum was loud enough for everyone to hear.

Is that what you want me to say, Princess?

Yetunde gripped Muna's wrist with fat fingers. Of course not, you foolish creature! The white is looking for a reason why the Master might have lost his temper with Abiola. You must convince her you waved your brother goodbye as he left the house.

I've already tried, Princess. She asked me the question while you and the Master were away, but she believes me too damaged to know what is true and what isn't.

Yetunde frowned in annoyance. How can you know what the white believes?

The Hausa speaker said I wasn't to worry if I couldn't remember everything, Princess. The white told her to say it wasn't my

31

fault if I didn't know which day the gardener came and Abiola went missing.

Yetunde's rings bit into her flesh. There's no '*and*' about it. The gardener comes on Wednesdays. Abiola went missing on Thursday.

I didn't know that, Princess. I've never seen the gardener. You don't allow me near the windows when he's working outside. You said you didn't want him to know I was here.

Yetunde took several deep breaths to calm herself. Did you tell the white the two things happened on Wednesday?

No, Princess. I said I didn't know which day they happened.

Yetunde thrust her away. You've made it worse, she said angrily. It's no wonder the white suspects the Master. He should have called a lawyer sooner. Mr Broadstone says she had no business talking to you without an adult present.

I wouldn't have answered any of her questions if the Hausa speaker hadn't said I had to, Princess. Some were very strange.

Such as?

Were you and the Master kind to me, Princess? Did you love me? Did I love you? I told her yes and made no mention of the cellar or the rod because I didn't want you to think me ungrateful.

Yetunde moved impatiently to the window. Were you asked why the Master took so long to summon the police on Thursday evening?

Yes, Princess.

What answer did you give?

None, Princess. I sat in silence, staring at my hands. The Hausa speaker said I didn't have to be afraid if I told the truth . . . but I was sure you wouldn't like it if I did. It might have seemed strange to them if I'd said you thought it more important to find me a dress than look for Abiola.

She watched the play of expressions on Yetunde's bloated, ugly face. Yetunde showed her emotions so openly, and Muna had lived with her so long, it wasn't hard to guess the thoughts that were running through her head. She wanted to doubt Muna's honesty but she couldn't. Her contempt for the girl's abilities was too ingrained to believe her capable of invention. It certainly didn't occur to her that Muna understood English, or that the knowledge she'd gained from listening to everything the white said allowed her to twist the truth.

Yetunde clenched her fists at her sides, releasing her frustration in a resentful sigh. We're being accused of things we haven't done, she said, and all because there are no CCTV images of Abiola on the day he went missing. The lawyer says we must find a way to prove he was alive. He told me to ask you which crisps and sweets you put in his lunch box that morning?

Muna wriggled her shoulders in pretended discomfort. I didn't put in any, Princess. Abiola stole all that were left when he came home from school the day before. He took them outside and ate them in the little house in the garden.

Yetunde glared at her. Why didn't you tell me?

You'd have beaten me, Princess. It made you angry when Abiola stole food.

Yetunde rattled her bracelets in annoyance. You're not to tell the white that. Say you put the crisps in his lunch box on Thursday. Better still, say you saw me doing it. What colour packets were they? How many? The police know the answer so be sure to remember accurately.

There were three red ones, Princess. Abiola kicked me because he only likes green and blue.

Why were the stores so low? I bought enough to last a month.

Abiola stole crisps every afternoon, Princess. If I tried to stop him, he hurt me. He wasn't a nice boy. I think the white knows you and the Master didn't like him either. She asked me twice why you don't weep for him more.

Yetunde's glare hardened. Can't she see our anguish?

I don't believe so, Princess. The Hausa speaker said the Master keeps trying to blame others for Abiola being missing . . . and men who do that want to hide their own guilt. She pressed me over and over again about whether he went out in his car between coming home and calling the police. I didn't know how to answer so I said nothing.

Wretched girl! You should have said he didn't.

Muna raised her head. But the white would have known I was lying, Princess. My mattress is not in the cellar any more, and only the Master could have taken it away. Will she not have pictures of the journey he made in his car? Will she not ask him if he took Abiola as well?

Five

Inspector Jordan informed the Songolis the next day that she was removing her team from the house. Ebuka and Yetunde greeted the news with relief, but not Muna whose naïve wish had been that the police stay for ever. Her sense of power had been very brief. Olubayo had been right, and she wrong, and despair overwhelmed her as she thought of being returned to the cellar.

It was Mr Broadstone's fault. He had refused the Inspector any further contact with his clients unless she produced evidence implicating them, and he guarded the Songolis closely to ensure that happened. It meant the Inspector never found out that Ebuka liked visiting whores, and her suspicion remained that he was responsible for his son's disappearance. Only the liaison officer said goodbye, giving a small wave as she left through the front door, and Muna knew her last chance of help had gone when it closed behind her.

Mr Broadstone tapped his watch, saying he had an appointment elsewhere, and then advised the Songolis in an undertone to be careful what they said and did. The police might have left but it didn't mean the investigation was over. There were ways and means of monitoring conversations and the Inspector had

had plenty of time to apply for permission to install listening devices in the house.

Ebuka took offence at the remark but he kept his voice low when he spoke. There was nothing they *could* say, he muttered, accusing the lawyer of not believing him and his wife when they said they were ignorant of what had happened to their son.

Mr Broadstone was unmoved. 'It's not my job to believe or disbelieve,' he answered drily. 'I merely take instructions. You asked me to get rid of the police and that's what I've done. It won't change anything. Your car, your computers and mobiles will still be examined and if anything untoward is found, you'll be arrested and asked for an explanation.'

'There is nothing.'

'I hope you're right. They'll be looking doubly hard at your car if they already know you went out again on Thursday evening between arriving home and giving them a call. They won't accept you were driving around the streets looking for Abiola if they find his DNA in the boot.'

'It's what most fathers would do,' Ebuka protested nervously. 'You said so yourself.'

Mr Broadstone lowered his voice even further. 'Indeed, but they don't forget to tell the police about it afterwards. You'd better pray the car wasn't captured on camera that time. You'll have a hard job persuading Inspector Jordan that such a reasonable excuse for a two-hour delay slipped the minds of both you *and* your wife.'

After he departed, the Songolis argued with each other in whispered Hausa. Each blamed the other for their problems. Yetunde said Ebuka should have known about street cameras. Ebuka said Yetunde should never have brought Muna into their house. But for her, they could have called the police immediately.

Neither said aloud that Muna had set her demons upon them, but their hate-filled glances in her direction told her that's what they believed. Nothing else could account for the chaos that had entered their lives. It was Yetunde's favourite sport to beat the Devil out of the girl, and Muna had come to welcome the punishment. If the Devil was so hard to expel, it meant He must be real.

Sometimes at night, in the darkness of the cellar, she heard Him whispering to her. His words were always encouraging. Muna was His chosen one. His beautiful one. His clever one. If she bided her time, He would prove to her how powerful He was. She had longed for Him to strike Ebuka dead each time the door at the top of the steps opened, or whip the rod from Yetunde's hand, but she saw now that He preferred to inflict a more lingering pain.

Ebuka had become a shadow of himself these last few days and Yetunde's overweening sense of importance was much deflated. Muna imagined they felt grief for Abiola – she had seen misery in both their faces from time to time – but it was fear of the police that troubled them more. Perhaps even fear of each other.

Their hostility was very strong, particularly where Muna was concerned. Ebuka said thieves reaped what they sowed. If Yetunde hadn't brazenly stolen another woman's child, she wouldn't have lost her son. He'd warned her at the time that no good could come of such an action. But Yetunde accused him of hypocrisy. Did he think she didn't know what went on in her house? Who would believe Ebuka was innocent of Abiola's fate if the girl ever spoke of the obscene acts he'd performed on her from the age of eight years old?

Muna sat as still as possible, hoping immobility would make her invisible. It was hard to pick up every word because their whispers were so low, but she trembled at the thought of the beatings she'd receive for being the cause of so much hatred. Yetunde's words suggested she knew that Ebuka visited Muna in the cellar, and Muna dreaded what the Master would do to her. He had said many times that she would learn the real meaning of pain if Princess ever found out.

Muna didn't doubt it was the Devil who jumped into Olubayo's body and caused him to behave as he did. Without warning, the boy fell to the floor, flinging his body from side to side as if demons were pricking him with red-hot needles. Yetunde howled in shock, screaming at Ebuka to do something, and the man rose clumsily to his feet as the boy's eyes rolled to the back of his head and foam frothed on his lips.

Neither noticed Muna slip quietly from the room. She hid in the kitchen, squatting in the shadows of her favourite corner, and tried to persuade herself to run away. There would be no mercy if Yetunde believed Muna had caused Olubayo to writhe and twitch. But the girl was more afraid of the world outside than she was of this house where the Devil lived. It was surely to help little Muna that He'd set his demons on Olubayo.

A bare few minutes passed before she heard the sound of a siren and wheels on the gravel. People entered the hall. A man urged Mr and Mrs Songoli to be calm. They could accompany their son to hospital but first he needed answers to some questions. Had Olubayo ever had a seizure before? How long had this one lasted? The voices were muted inside the sitting room, but it wasn't long before feet tramped through the hall, the front door closed and silence blanketed the house.

Muna listened to the vanishing wail of the siren as it disappeared into the distance. Had all the Songolis gone? she wondered. Was she alone in the house for the first time since Abiola vanished? She rose to her feet and stood at the closed kitchen door, straining to hear footsteps or breathing. She waited through an interminable space of time before carefully easing the handle on the door and tiptoeing into the hall.

She saw Ebuka emerge from the sitting room but had no time to retreat. He was upon her in a single step, catching her round the throat with his forearm and clamping a hand across her mouth before she could cry out. Her terror was so great that she prayed for death.

He hissed the same words into her ear that he always used. *Bitch . . . Whore . . .Temptress . . . Polluter of men . . .* But they meant no more to Muna now than when she lay on her blood-soaked mattress, unable to move beneath his weight. All she knew was that they were the precursor to unendurable suffering.

His arm was hooked too tightly around her neck, robbing her of breath, and her mind grew dark. It meant she had few clear memories of what happened next. She remembered the light coming on at the top of the cellar steps, remembered her knees folding beneath her as she slipped from Ebuka's grasp. But the rest was a series of half-formed images. She saw the black bowels of the earth open before her, felt Ebuka being lifted over her by a giant fist, watched his body tumbling down the steps.

More clearly than anything, she heard the Devil laugh.

She dreamed of Abiola. He stood at a distance from her, his hands cupped in a begging gesture. He called to Muna for help but she turned away to look at children playing in a sunlit courtyard. It was a strange dream. When she looked back, her eyes were open, the tufts of the hall carpet caressed her cheek, and she was staring down the cellar steps at Ebuka.

She lay for a long time, watching him. He wasn't dead, which she thought a pity, but he didn't seem able to move. One of his legs was twisted beneath him, the table had fallen over, trapping his arm, and his head was jammed between two of Yetunde's trunks. She gazed impassively into his wide-open eyes, noting curiously how his expression alternated between fear and pleading.

She rose when he began to threaten her with Yetunde's anger if she failed to help him. She crept down the steps and squatted in the dust beside him. Close to, his fear was very strong.

I can't feel anything, he whispered. My arms and legs don't work.

Muna made no response. She had more patience than Ebuka and could stare at him for hours if necessary.

As time passed, he grew angry with her. *Do* something, he ordered. *Do* something . . . *do* something . . .

What, Master? she asked when it finally pleased her to answer him.

Use the telephone. Dial 999. Request an ambulance as we did for Olubayo.

I don't know how to, Master, and no one would understand me if I could.

Then bring me my mobile and hold it to my mouth while I speak.

I can't, Master. The white took every telephone in the house except the one attached by wire to the wall in the sitting room.

Ebuka's tongue flickered across dry, nervous lips. Go to the front gate, he begged. There are men out there with cameras. Bring one of them to me.

Princess doesn't allow me to show myself to strangers, Master. She'll beat me with the rod if I disobey her.

She'll beat you harder if you leave me to die. Are you too stupid to understand that?

Muna found it strange that his mouth and eyes worked when nothing else did. She touched a finger to one of his hands and felt how cold it was. Princess wouldn't want a man with a camera down here, Master. He'll ask what made you fall down the steps and show pictures of you on the television . . . and people will wonder why you stayed behind to look in the cellar instead of going to the hospital with Olubayo. I expect Princess and the white will wonder also.

Ebuka's eyes widened as if he were realising for the first time that he didn't really know this girl. It was the longest speech he'd ever heard her make. It doesn't matter, he insisted. I need help. Are you so lacking in human feeling that you can't see that?

I am what you and Princess have made me, Master. The feelings I have are the ones you've taught me. If they aren't human the fault is yours.

Muna fancied she saw horror in his face.

You're a monster, he grated from his dry mouth. Your demons have brought this evil to my family.

Muna didn't answer. He was tiring rapidly and she waited until his breathing was so shallow she could barely see the rise and fall of his chest. She went upstairs to collect the duvet from Yetunde's bed and a glass of water from the kitchen, placed them solicitously over and beside Ebuka, and then resumed her position next to him.

When she heard the front door open, and Yetunde's heavy tread on the floor above, she took Ebuka's hand in hers and cried loudly for Princess to come to the cellar.

AUTUMN

Six

Muna's view of the world was a simple one. Things happened because they were meant to happen, and nothing she did or didn't do could alter what fate had ordained. It disappointed her that Ebuka lived but she took comfort when she learned from Yetunde that he'd broken his back. She had faith that the Devil intended him to suffer.

He was absent from the house for many weeks and Yetunde swung between hope and despair about his condition. When movement returned to his hands and arms, she believed he would rise from his bed and walk again. When the doctors told her he would be in a wheelchair for the rest of his life, she became depressed and cried every day about the difficulties they would face if Ebuka were unable to work.

Muna avoided her on these occasions, preferring to resume her duties than wait in idleness for Yetunde's sorrow to turn in a flash from misery to anger. Yetunde wanted someone to blame and Muna's lack of expression infuriated her. Only a girl beset by demons would be so uncaring about Olubayo having to leave his private school or the dreaded prospect of Ebuka being sent home when the hospital decided there was no more they could do for him.

Yetunde would have forced Muna back into the cellar if she could but her fear of the police stopped her. She no longer believed there were listening devices in the house but she was wary of doing anything to make them suspicious. Inspector Jordan made frequent appearances, using the excuse of needing to clarify evidence, but she always came without warning.

The lawyer, Mr Broadstone, was the most regular visitor. At the beginning, his reports were about the investigation into Abiola's disappearance. The police had found no suspicious DNA in the boot of Ebuka's car although they'd lifted dust and fibres that matched sweepings they'd taken from the cellar. Since even Ebuka's doctors wouldn't allow him to be interviewed, Mr Broadstone had given explanations on his client's behalf. When he repeated them to Yetunde, she clapped her hands in approval, saying Ebuka could never have argued his case so well.

Mr Broadstone had told the police that Mr Songoli's work required him to travel from time to time. His last trip – recorded in his office diary – had been five days before Abiola's disappearance. Because Mr Songoli stored his luggage in the cellar, any case or overnight bag which he placed in his boot would carry dust and fibre from the cellar floor. Forensic scientists might argue that this wouldn't account for the quantity found, but a jury would always give a grieving father the benefit of the doubt.

And grief was certainly what Mr Songoli had felt on the night of Abiola's disappearance. It was why he had omitted to say he'd driven the streets in a desperate search for the boy after coming home that Thursday evening. Mr Broadstone described his client as a proud man who couldn't admit how deep his despair was when he failed to find his son. His wife looked to him for strength yet, blinded by tears, he had pulled into the side of the road and wept uncontrollably for over an hour before returning to call the police.

Mr Broadstone never described Ebuka's accident as a blessing in disguise, but he mentioned several times that public sympathy had swung behind the Songolis. The people of this country were soft-hearted, he said, and there was a sense of collective guilt that visitors to their shores had suffered so much. To lose Abiola – without his body being found or any progress made in the police investigation – was bad enough; but for Mr Songoli to miss his footing on the cellar steps seemed to compound the tragedy. It wasn't right that a man, distracted by worry and grief, should be asked to produce insurance documents from his files in the cellar to prove his other son was entitled to medical treatment.

'The British pride themselves on their free healthcare system,' he told Yetunde. 'It embarrasses them when the press and media run stories like this. We may have a case for compensation if we can claim your husband was so intimidated by the paramedics that he put finding documents before his own safety.'

Yetunde looked doubtful. 'Is that what he told you happened?'

'He said he was afraid Olubayo would receive poor treatment without proof of insurance. I'm assuming the paramedics led him to believe that?'

Yetunde's expression said he was wrong, but honesty was less important to her than money. 'Will we be paid if they did?'

'Paraplegia is a serious disability, Mrs Songoli. Your husband should receive a substantial amount if we can prove the paramedics were at fault.' Mr Broadstone leaned forward. 'Perhaps they led him to believe Olubayo would be denied treatment? Perhaps you believed the same thing and begged him in Hausa to find the insurance policy and rush with it to the hospital?'

'We spoke only in English. The ambulance men know that.'

'It'll be their word against yours.'

Yetunde shook her head. 'They allowed me to ride in the front with the driver and I heard him speak on the radio to the hospital. He said he had a thirteen-year-old male patient with a suspected epileptic seizure but made no mention of papers. Whoever took that call will side with them against us.'

'That won't affect how your husband felt about the situation. Just by being asked for your names and nationality, he will have felt under pressure. I'm sure you can recall him looking anxious as you left.'

Yetunde thought for a moment. 'He became angry when we were told that only one of us could accompany Olubayo. He had an argument with the driver, saying the police had impounded his car and he had no means of following without it. The man answered that he didn't make the rules and warned Ebuka that it was an offence to threaten a member of the emergency services.'

'Had Mr Songoli raised his hand?'

Yetunde nodded.

'He's a passionate man from a different culture. It's natural for him to express anxiety through hand gestures. No official in uniform should have accused him of committing an offence because of it . . . particularly when he was so clearly distressed about Olubayo's seizure.'

Yetunde brightened. 'Will we be given money if I say that?'

'It'll help.'

After that all Mr Broadstone's visits involved talk of compensation. He was white yet everything he said was against whites, and Muna distrusted him for it. Did he hate his own tribe so much that he was willing to teach Princess to steal from them? As time wore on, he persuaded Yetunde to think about suing the police.

The investigation into Abiola's disappearance remained open but no progress was being made. Mr Broadstone suggested this was Inspector Jordan's fault for ignoring other leads to focus her team's attention on Mr Songoli. At the minimum, she should have ordered her people to interview all known paedophiles in the area and check CCTV footage to track their cars as assiduously as they'd tracked Ebuka's.

For the most part, Muna learned of these things from the conversations Yetunde had with Olubayo in the evenings. The boy was as poor a learner as his brother had been, and Yetunde had to explain the details several times. She took pleasure in blaming Ebuka for their problems – they wouldn't have to count their pennies if he hadn't been careless enough to fall down the cellar steps – and Olubayo soon developed a bitter contempt for his crippled father.

He was taking pills for his epilepsy and they gave him headaches and made him irritable. He claimed his life was over when Yetunde removed him from his private school because the fees were too expensive. He brooded on his grievances in his bedroom during the summer holidays, but expressed them physically when he began his new school in the autumn. Every afternoon, he came home and raged in anger because his father had made him a laughing stock.

He complained to Yetunde that he had no friends and was bullied mercilessly by the other pupils. They called him a 'fucktard' because of his epilepsy, said his father was a 'spaz' for being in a wheelchair and his abducted brother 'paedo-bait'. Even the teachers were unkind, taking him to task for being aggressive instead of expelling any boy or girl who teased him.

The stress and emotion played havoc with his seizures. When he wasn't writhing on the floor, he was in hospital having his medication adjusted. Yetunde had no patience with him, claiming her life was worse than his. Her dreams of happiness had never included a cripple for a husband or an epileptic for a son.

Muna remained a mute witness to everything. Stillness and silence had served her well over the years. To draw attention to herself was to invite pain. Nevertheless she saw how frustrated and angry both Princess and Olubayo were becoming, and she prepared herself for when their rage turned on her.

Olubayo was the first to threaten her. He appeared in the kitchen doorway one afternoon with the rod in his hand. My father will never be able to wield this again, he told her, smacking it against his palm. That makes me the man of the house. You must do as I say or be punished.

Muna was rinsing a heavy saucepan under the tap. He'll be angry when he returns and discovers you've tried to take his place, she said.

I'm not afraid of him. He's lost his strength. His mind is as weak as his body. All he does is weep in shame each time the nurses remove the bags that collect his urine and faeces.

Muna held the saucepan in front of her as she dried it with a towel. There are more ways to discipline a son than by the rod. If the Master chooses, he can order Princess to lock you in the cellar and let the demons tear at you the way they tore at him.

You lie.

I heard them laugh as he fell. The sound was so loud it carried upstairs. It's a place of evil. Your father was foolish to enter.

Then I'll push you in there and let them tear at you.

They won't harm me. I heard them whispering in the walls when I lived in darkness, and they said it was your family they want to destroy, not me. Do you think Abiola would be lost or your father crippled if the demons bore them no ill will?

Olubayo looked nervous. Whites say there are no such things as demons.

Princess believes in them and so does the Master, Muna answered. When I found the courage to creep back down to see what had happened, his eyes – so big and round with terror – told me so. He knew they were taking payment for the bad things he and Princess have done to me. They'll come for you, ugly boy, if you think to hurt me . . . and next time they'll do more than make your body writhe on the floor and foam spill from your lips.

She vibrated her tongue against her palate to produce a snakelike hiss and felt a satisfying fulfilment when Olubayo fled across the hall and up the stairs to his room. He would do what he did every night, sit before his screen, pulling at himself and grunting like a pig. It's what made him stupid.

It was another week before Yetunde took the rod to Muna. She'd been content to leave the girl alone as long as she performed her duties. Mr Broadstone's visits, and the occasional unannounced appearance by Inspector Jordan or the police liaison officer, persuaded her to keep calling Muna her daughter and allowing her to wear floral prints instead of black.

At the outset of the investigation, she'd ordered several dresses in Muna's size out of fear the police would notice the girl always wore a kaba that was too big for her. Later, she seemed to feel they might as well be put to use, or perhaps she'd even come to prefer a servant who could be seen by strangers, for she allowed Muna to open the front door when the bell rang and bring trays of tea and sugared almonds to the sitting room.

In front of visitors, she always thanked Muna prettily on these occasions, calling her a good girl or a kind girl, but Muna suspected it galled her to do it. Every so often she caught a flash of enmity in Yetunde's eyes as if she were contrasting Muna's improved circumstances with her own diminished ones.

Her temper came to the boil one morning when Muna failed to make shortbread biscuits as sweet as she liked. A torrent of pent-up abuse poured from her mouth. She accused Muna of everything from murdering Abiola, attempting the same with Ebuka and causing Olubayo's seizure before seizing her by the arm and dragging her to the kitchen. You'll not get up this time, she warned, flinging Muna to the floor and taking up the rod.

Muna twisted on to her back and cried out as loudly as she could. If you do this, the white will believe you did the same to Abiola, Princess. This is the day the gardener comes. He'll hear my screams and repeat what I say to the police.

It was enough to stay Yetunde's hand.

This is what I will shout, Princess. 'No, Mamma, no. I have done no wrong. Please don't kill me the way you killed my brother. You can't beat two children to death and hope to escape punishment.'

Yetunde's eyes blazed. What lies are these? Who taught you to speak them in English?

I learned them from the white, Princess. She told the Hausa speaker she believes it was you who took Abiola's life. She will know it for certain if you take mine.

Seven

Autumn was well advanced by the time Ebuka came home from hospital. The flowers were dying and the trees that lined the street had turned from gold to russet red. Since the gardener left, the grass on the lawn had become wild and unkempt, and weeds grew in the beds that lined the gravel drive.

Yetunde had dismissed the man on the day Muna had drawn attention to him, claiming she couldn't afford him. Muna had watched his departure with regret. In truth, she doubted he would have heard her if she'd called from inside the house, or taken notice if he had – he seemed overly timid when speaking to Yetunde – but his presence had saved her from a beating.

She plotted other ways to protect herself from Yetunde's anger. Ways that came to her at night in dreams so real that she knew the Devil had not abandoned her. She hid weapons in each room of the house – knives from the kitchen, a hammer and a chisel from Ebuka's toolbox, Abiola's cricket and baseball bats, a heavy doorstop – and made sure she could remember where they were.

She practised using the telephone whenever Yetunde went out by studying the keypad and listening to the buzzing noise against her ear when she lifted the receiver. Dial 999, Ebuka had said. Muna knew nine was a number from watching Abiola count on his fingers, and she guessed it must be one of the buttons on the keypad, but she didn't know which or how often she should press it.

She tried them all, pressing once, then twice, then three times. Most of her efforts resulted in silence or a voice saying 'the number you have dialled has not been recognised', but when she pressed one button on the right-hand side three times, she was answered immediately.

A thrill ran through her body when a woman's voice asked her which emergency service she required. Muna stood transfixed for several seconds; then she replaced the receiver and memorised the button she'd pressed. She was astonished at how quickly the woman had answered, how clear the voice had been and how easily she'd understood the words. It gave her hope that if she managed to reach the telephone before Yetunde, someone would help her.

Nevertheless, it wasn't long before she realised such a call would be pointless if she couldn't tell the woman where she was. There were houses for as far as she could see from the upstairs windows. How would a stranger know she was in this one? She pictured Yetunde laughing and pulling the telephone from her hand if all she could say was, 'Please help me. My name is Muna.'

If she'd known how to read, she could have looked at the envelopes that came through the door from time to time. But such a skill was beyond her. All she could do was wait and listen. Sooner or later, Yetunde would order something to be delivered to the house and Muna would remember what she said. It had never seemed necessary before. What was the point of learning the name of a street when she didn't even know which town she was in?

Her opportunity came when Yetunde ordered a taxi to collect Ebuka from his rehabilitation centre. He would require one that could take a wheelchair, and, no, she would not be accompanying him. If Mr Songoli needed help the driver would have to assist him. She gave an address that Muna heard and committed to her memory. It made no sense to her but she practised the words in her head over and over again. Twenty Three Fortis Row En Ten.

Yetunde had been speaking sourly of Ebuka's return for days. On Jeremy Broadstone's advice, she had ordered Ebuka to pretend he had only partial feeling in his hands and was unable to dress or feed himself, for the worse his injuries the higher the compensation would be. The plan seemed to have worked when Ebuka's consultant ordered him to be moved to a specialist centre thirty miles away where he was cared for at the taxpayers' expense. According to Mr Broadstone, this demonstrated that the Health Service was acknowledging fault for their patient's condition.

Yetunde couldn't have been happier. Ebuka's employer had agreed to pay his salary for six months until the nature of his disability was fully determined, Mr Broadstone's legal suits were progressing well, and she could indulge her laziness to her heart's content. Even Ebuka didn't require her to make a sixty-mile round trip to visit him when she couldn't drive. And this was a mercy, she confided to the lawyer, because her husband had lost his attraction for her.

She didn't like men with withered legs who wept continuously about their situation. Was it her fault he'd fallen down the cellar steps? Of course not, so how could he ask her to pick up the pieces afterwards by learning to change his catheter bags, keep his circulation working and his back and buttocks free of pressure sores? She shuddered every time she spoke of Ebuka's incontinence. It was unreasonable to expect a woman of her class to deal with such things.

To Muna's eyes, Yetunde found Jeremy Broadstone a great deal more desirable than Ebuka. She preened herself in front of the mirror when she knew he was coming, and found playful reasons to touch him when she showed him to a seat or handed him a cup of tea. It was harder to read Mr Broadstone, though Muna thought she saw distaste in his eyes each time Yetunde pushed another sugared almond or cream-filled bun into her already bloated face.

Idleness had made her fatter. She claimed she was comfort-eating out of grief for Abiola but Mr Broadstone suggested it might be better to show her grief in more obvious ways. She must learn to cross her hands over her heart each time his name was mentioned, produce tears on demand and whisper in a quavering voice when she spoke of the day he went missing. These were the reactions that judges and juries expected from mothers, and she needed to win their sympathy if her case against the police were to be successful.

Muna wondered why Mr Broadstone cared so much about Yetunde receiving payment until Olubayo asked his mother how much he would earn from the settlement. Too much, Yetunde told him. It was a bad system that said those who suffered pain and bereavement could only be recompensed through the efforts of lawyers. Mr Broadstone hardly needed the money – he was wealthy already – but he'd be paid handsomely if they won their case.

Muna knew then that Jeremy Broadstone was a false and shallow man. He was paying attention to Yetunde on a promise of money, which meant his smiles were insincere and his sympathy a pretence. And that pleased her. For all the powder Princess brushed on her face, the perfume she sprayed on her neck and the time she spent on her hair, the skinny white didn't like her enough to show compassion for free.

As the hour of Ebuka's arrival drew close, Yetunde's frustrations boiled over. With Olubayo at school, she expressed them openly to Muna. This wasn't fair. She'd never wanted to be Ebuka Songoli's wife. Her parents had arranged the marriage without ever asking her if she could learn to love him. She had tolerated him all these years because he went to work and earned good money, but she couldn't abide to spend every day in his company.

It was bad enough that she'd had to share a bed with Ebuka and allow him to maul her whenever the mood took him, but to have to clean his private parts and deal with the stench of his faeces and urine . . . The idea was abhorrent to her. She couldn't do it. If it had been in her power, she'd have refused responsibility for him and left him where he was. This vile country was to blame for the ills that had befallen him. Let the English assume his care instead of insisting that his wife must do it.

Muna waited until the tirade began to falter. I can care for the Master, Princess, she said quietly. It'll be no different from cleaning Abiola. Smells worry me less than they worry you.

But instead of being grateful, Yetunde eyed her suspiciously. Do you hope to make me look bad?

No, Princess. I thought only to help you. Perhaps the Master won't agree to my tending him. He may not want to be touched in his secret places by a girl.

Don't pretend you haven't done it before, Yetunde snapped. In any case he has no say in the matter. He must accept whatever arrangements I put in place. It's high time he learned how badly he's impoverished us through his stupidity.

Of course Yetunde pretended love when Ebuka arrived, running to plant juicy kisses on his cheeks inside the large, sliding-door taxi, but she did nothing to assist him out of it or into the wheelchair that the driver removed from the other side. The man was white-haired and elderly, and he eyed Yetunde cynically for a moment before asking her to move aside so that he could ease Ebuka from the seat to the chair. When he saw that she had no intention of helping her husband over the doorstep into the house either, he did that too, nodding to Muna who was standing in the shadows at the side of the hall.

He tapped Ebuka's shoulder. 'I'll leave you with your daughter, sir,' he said. 'I hope things go well for you. They generally do once you're in your own environment.'

A tear glistened in Ebuka's eye as he thanked the man for his kindness. What a sorry sight he was, Muna thought. So small and hunched in the wheelchair, his beard and hair tinged with grey and his skin a shade lighter from being inside for so long. She glanced towards Yetunde, who was arguing with the driver about the fare, and then walked forward to push Ebuka into the dining room.

Princess said you must sleep in here, Master. She made Olubayo and me bring Abiola's bed from upstairs because it won't matter if you mess it. I've put the same rubber sheet on that he always used.

Are you laughing at me?

No, Master. I haven't learned how to do that yet. Shall I leave you here or would you like to go somewhere else?

Tell Princess to come. I need help.

Muna moved round to look at him. She won't give it, Master. Your smell offends her. She liked it better when you were in hospital.

Will a nurse come?

No, Master. Princess is too poor to pay people to help you. You must look after yourself or let me do it.

He seemed more frightened now than he'd been in the cellar when he discovered he couldn't move. Muna stooped to look into his eyes.

You must learn courage and cleverness, Master. You'll not survive being the prisoner of people who despise you otherwise. Princess's temper is very uncertain. If you demand too much or your complaints irritate her, she will open the cellar door and push you down the steps.

Perhaps Ebuka thought she was talking about herself because he grasped the wheels of the chair and manoeuvred it backwards. Stay away from me, he warned with a tremor in his voice. Only you would do such a thing.

Not I, Master, but the same isn't true of Princess and Olubayo. You brought misfortune to them when you brought it to yourself, and they blame you for it.

And you do not?

No, Master. As your life gets worse, mine gets better. I thank you more often than I blame you. Shall I ask Princess to come or would you rather show me how to help you? You will find me a faster and more patient learner. Princess is too lazy to do anything well.

Eight

Muna wondered if all people were like the Songolis. It was hard to tell when her contact with strangers was so limited. She took what she could from the television but Yetunde's diet of soap operas, American movies and chat shows were as full of anger and aggression as the woman who watched them.

Sometimes Muna saw love portrayed on the screen when men and women tore off their clothes and grunted like Ebuka and Olubayo, or mothers caressed their children and said they loved them, but she remained unmoved by such scenes. The gestures and words were always the same, as if there were only two ways to express affection.

Yet as time wore on she noticed that Ebuka's eyes softened each time she entered his room. It made her curious because it seemed to indicate a feeling for her that he'd never had before. She might have feared it was lust if Yetunde hadn't delighted in flicking his flaccid penis and telling him he'd never be able to go with white whores again.

To see him naked disgusted Yetunde but Muna felt only indifference. He had lost his power to hurt her, and the withered muscles of his legs made him seem shrunken and puny.

Occasionally she wished she'd been able to see his penis when he came at her in the darkness of the cellar. She'd have been less frightened if she'd known what it was he was thrusting into her hole and her mouth. It was such a poor little thing and she had strong teeth. She could have bitten it off and spat it out along with his filth.

For the first few days Ebuka closed his eyes and refused to speak when she came to his room. It mattered little to Muna. She had been silent so long that talking was a burden. She was happier living inside her head than moving her stiff, reluctant mouth to form words.

Her thoughts on Ebuka were always about revenge. Sometimes she was in the mood to kill him. It would be so easy to take the bag of faeces, snip off the end and force him to choke on his own excrement. It would be payback for the slime he'd emptied into her mouth, and the idea appealed to her. But the Devil whispered caution and patience. Muna's circumstances would change for the worse if Ebuka died and Mr Broadstone stopped coming to the house. The lawyer's visits and promises of money were the only curb on Yetunde's temper.

Ebuka spoke eventually because he hadn't the patience to stay quiet for ever. Perhaps he found Muna's attention to his welfare puzzling for he asked if she was glad he'd lived. She told him she was, and he gave a hollow laugh, reminding her of what she'd said in the cellar. What had changed? Did she hate him less now that he was a cripple? She assured him her feelings remained the same. Her gladness was to see him as much a prisoner as she was, and this pleasure would have been denied her if he'd died.

Ready tears filled his eyes. So your dislike of me remains the same yet you show more kindness than my wife does. Why?

Princess will make us both suffer if I don't, Master. She needs you to live because she wants the money Mr Broadstone says he can win for her.

Is everything you do done out of fear of a beating?

You know it is, Master.

The tears spilled down his cheeks. I've had a long time to think about the day of the accident, Muna. I behaved badly. Will you accept how deeply I've come to regret my treatment of you? Can you forgive me for the things I've done in the past?

If you wish it, Master.

Muna marvelled at how much easier he seemed in his mind after this exchange, as if words alone could make him better. He wept less frequently, put more effort into his rehabilitation and thanked her constantly for her efforts. Once or twice he begged her for a smile and, out of curiosity to see his reaction, she made the attempt. Even the smallest twitch of her lips brought a beam in response; and how odd that was, she thought. Did he think her curved mouth any more sincere than her forgiveness?

Muna knew full well that his regrets were for himself. If nothing had happened to change the course of his family's life, he would still be coming to her in the darkness of the cellar. But it suited her to reward him with little smiles for it gave her a renewed sense of power to see his face light up when she entered the room.

She became skilful at pushing down on his bladder to empty it, managing his catheters and bags and keeping his skin free of pressure sores. She helped him perform his daily upper-body exercises to increase the strength in his arms, hands and neck, and lifted and moved his legs to maintain the circulation of blood through his veins. Once a week, a district nurse came to monitor his progress, always ushered in by Yetunde, and each time the nurse told Ebuka he was doing well before congratulating him on his devoted wife.

Muna loved to see the discord these statements created between the Songolis after the nurse left. They argued heatedly, Ebuka accusing Yetunde of taking compliments she hadn't earned and Yetunde accusing Ebuka of ruining their chances of compensation. It was his duty to play up his disability, she stormed. He was of no use to her and Olubayo if he couldn't win money for them.

In turn this led to arguments about Yetunde's profligate spending habits. Ebuka was furious at how depleted their reserves had become while he was in hospital. He didn't care how wretched Yetunde had been after Abiola's disappearance. He called her greedy and stupid, saying only a fool would indulge her appetites on a solicitor's promise to win a lawsuit. Had she no sense? No restraint? Must her happiness always come first?

Such confrontations never ended well for him. He was left to hurl insults at a closed door after Yetunde walked from the room, taunting him for being a cripple. He grew fonder of Muna each time this happened, mistaking her quiet resumption of his exercises for kindness rather than a desire to avoid Princess. Yetunde's rage was always worse when the nurse said Ebuka was showing improvement.

Yet why this was so, Muna didn't know. With her own ears, she had heard Jeremy Broadstone tell Yetunde how important it was to follow the regime she'd been given for Ebuka. The doctors would become suspicious if they didn't see a slow but steady improvement in his mental and physical condition when the legal suit argued that Mrs Songoli had put her life on hold to provide full-time care. She must prove how dedicated she was, how many hours a day she was sacrificing to looking after her husband, how impossible it was for her to seek employment when his needs came first.

'It's Mr Songoli who'll be awarded the compensation,' he reminded her, 'so you must keep him and his doctors happy if you want control of the money.'

Yetunde pulled a sour face. 'It's a shame he didn't break his neck. We'd get more if he was completely paralysed.'

'And you'd be expected to use it to pay for an army of trained nurses to tend him round the clock. Quadriplegia is a serious condition. This way you have the best of both worlds. The cushion of invested income and a husband who, over time, can learn to cope with his disability and achieve some independence.'

'If he doesn't, I'll put him in a home. I can't be at his beck and call for ever.'

Muna recalled this conversation weeks later when Yetunde stood for several minutes in the doorway of the dining room, watching her lift and move Ebuka's legs. Yetunde's dislike of what she was seeing was so palpable that Muna could feel it across the space between them. She peeped through her lashes at Yetunde's purple face and watched her lips mouth angrily that she was going out.

She waited until she heard the front door close. Why is Princess cross with us, Master? she asked, gently rotating Ebuka's left ankle. Doesn't she want you to get better?

She's jealous.

What does that mean, Master?

She knows I prefer your help to hers. It makes her feel unwanted.

Is that a bad thing, Master?

64

It is if you think you're important.

Is Princess important, Master?

Not as much as she'd like to be.

Muna moved to the other side of the bed to rotate his right ankle. She longs for Mr Broadstone to think her important, Master. She paints her face for hours before he comes.

She wants the compensation he can win for us. We'll have nothing to live on otherwise.

Princess wants the money for herself, Master. She signed papers for Mr Broadstone while you were in hospital. He said they would make her rich.

He meant all of us.

I don't think so, Master.

Ebuka watched as she smoothed lotion into the unfeeling skin of his left calf. Are you as jealous as she is? he asked. Are you trying to set me against her?

I ask only that you show wisdom, Master.

What kind of wisdom?

The sort that tells you Princess is greedy, Master. She wants your money more than she wants you . . . and when she has it, she'll keep the nurse from the house.

For what reason?

To make your life shorter. If no one sees you, she can be as cruel as she likes.

A frown of uncertainty creased Ebuka's brow. She wouldn't dare harm me. My doctors will ask questions.

She dared it with me, Master. Any of her beatings could have killed me, and no one would have known. I didn't exist until the police came to the house on the day Abiola went missing.

WINTER

Nine

As the days shortened and sleet rattled the window panes, Muna would have been frightened to go to her room if she hadn't discovered that the key to Abiola's door also locked hers. Several times she squatted in the corner, listening to the whisper of naked feet on the carpet of the corridor, watching the handle turn and hearing Yetunde's breath exhale against the panels.

To Muna's eyes, jealousy was a strange and complicated emotion. Yetunde hated Ebuka, and wanted nothing to do with his care, but she couldn't bear to see Muna perform the tasks instead. Ebuka hated Yetunde, and was only truly happy when she was absent, but he reserved his softest smiles for Muna when Yetunde was in the room.

The concept was a mystery to Muna since she had no feelings for either of them. Their antagonism reminded her of Olubayo's fights with Abiola whenever the younger boy stole the older boy's clothes, and she wondered if jealousy had more to do with possessions than with love. Perhaps Yetunde thought Ebuka belonged to her? This was a curious idea when the only person Yetunde had ever laid claim to was Muna. You are mine to treat as I like, she had said each time she raised the rod.

But when Ebuka finally decided to leave his room, Yetunde's wrath became worse. Out of sight was out of mind but to watch Ebuka tease smiles from Muna's solemn face, and call her pretty, drove her to distraction. She was angriest in the evenings when Ebuka sat in the kitchen, watching Muna prepare supper and complimenting her on her skills. She would make a good wife, he said often in Yetunde's hearing.

Olubayo did nothing to lessen the tension between his parents. Having refused to enter Ebuka's room for weeks, he now preferred to join his father in the kitchen rather than sit with Yetunde in front of the television. He too appeared to be jealous of Ebuka's new-found affection for Muna and showed it in the efforts he made to win his father's approval. Had Muna been capable of sympathy she might have pitied his clumsy attempts, which were rebuffed more often than they were appreciated.

Muna never questioned Ebuka's behaviour, only Yetunde's and Olubayo's. She despised them for their stupidity, wondering why they couldn't see that Ebuka was acting deliberately to make their turmoil worse. She assumed it made him feel powerful to stoke up Yetunde's anger and have Olubayo beg for his attention because the idea that it pleased him to sit with her never crossed her mind.

Muna had no desire to be in another's company. Closeness was something to fear and avoid. She preferred to squat in a corner alone. Listening.

Yetunde was tipped into a frenzy when Ebuka asked Muna to take him into the garden. She watched sullenly as he told Muna to put on one of Abiola's anoraks which hung in the downstairs cloakroom and the wellington boots that stood beneath it. Muna said they were too big for her and that she wasn't ready to go outside. She had never left the house and the cold and the rain frightened her. But Ebuka would have none of it and cajoled her into taking the anorak from the hook.

She did as he asked because he said he'd go on his own otherwise, and she had a greater fear of being left with Yetunde. Nevertheless, her terror of the outside was genuine. Had she known what brainwashing was, she would have understood why, since Yetunde's worst thrashings were associated with it. She had beaten Muna mercilessly each time she'd caught her staring out of a window or daring to open the kitchen door to allow a breeze to dispel the heat.

Perhaps it was seeing Muna in her son's clothes that caused Yetunde to erupt, or simple fury at her having her orders overturned, but her flailing charge caught Muna by surprise. She would have been knocked to the ground if one of Yetunde's massive hands had smacked her head instead of gripping the sleeve of the anorak. If she thought to stop Muna escaping her, she had forgotten how thin the girl was, for her fingers caught only cloth, and Muna was out of the garment even before Yetunde had drawn a breath.

She backed towards the stairs, watching warily as Yetunde stormed and screeched in the middle of the hall. Was Ebuka ignorant of the embarrassment he had caused her by becoming a cripple? Did he care nothing for his family's pride that he was willing to parade himself in public? Worse, to allow the ugly piccaninny to accompany him? Did he have no shame?

The shame is yours, Ebuka said. It's you who sees me as a cripple and you who stole this child. I've asked you many times to mend your ignorance but you'd rather eat bonbons than put your mind to learning. It makes you as unattractive to me as I am to you.

Her demons have taken you over, Yetunde cried.

The demons are in your head where they've always been, woman. You hold to them because they give you an excuse for cruelty.

Yetunde quivered from head to toe, so intense was her emotion. You never denied them before.

Only through weakness. You're easier to live with when you get your own way. If demons exist, they're in you . . . not in this unfortunate girl.

She's poisoned you against me.

Not so, Ebuka growled. My feelings for you haven't changed since the day we married.

Then why do you look at me with such hatred?

Because I'm done with pretence. There was never any love between us. We were ill matched from the start and joy has been absent from my life ever since. You taught my sons to be as greedy and lazy as you, and now one is gone and the other epileptic. What is left for me to have pride in?

Muna watched in puzzlement as Yetunde rocked to and fro in grief at this statement. Her distress seemed genuine yet Muna could see no reason for it. Had she not expressed similar sentiments herself when she said she'd never wanted Ebuka for a husband? And had she not criticised Olubayo constantly for being feeble-minded?

Yetunde's distress turned to anger again. You'll not divorce me, she snapped. I'll see this girl dead before I let her steal you from me.

Ebuka gave a contemptuous shake of his head before wheeling himself to where she'd dropped the anorak on the floor. Muna saw Yetunde clench her fists as he leaned forward to pick it up, and she called a shout of warning. But she was too late. Yetunde took a step forward and slammed both hands on the back of her husband's neck, using her weight to topple him from his seat and send the chair spinning backwards.

Muna had pictured moments like this a hundred times in her imagination. She had rehearsed every action she might have to take, in whichever room she was in, when the day came for her to defend herself. It was sweet chance that it was happening here in the hall since this was her preferred place. She turned the handle of the cellar door and pushed it open before slipping round the wall behind the woman's back.

Yetunde had forgotten Muna, so intent was she on damaging Ebuka. When she wasn't kicking his head, she was stamping on his arms as he tried to drag himself away from her feet. She laughed and laughed, and Muna was sure her wits had gone. Her great bulk seemed to tremble with delight each time a whimper of pain came from her husband's mouth.

Muna reached the mahogany sideboard which stood outside the sitting-room door and retrieved the hammer that she'd hidden behind a large portrait photograph of Yetunde. Had she been taller and stronger she would have practised in her mind how to bring the weapon down on Yetunde's skull, but she was too frail to do anything so gratifying and had long since decided that her purpose would be better served by causing Yetunde to fall.

She knew her life would be forfeit unless Yetunde was too badly injured to retaliate so her dreams of these fights were bloody and violent. They played across her sleeping mind like the movies she saw on television. She had a particular fondness for the scenes where she drove a chisel again and again into Yetunde's breast or dropped to her knees to slam the doorstop repeatedly on to the hand wielding the rod until she knew from the pulpy squelch of the flesh that it could never be used again.

Yet she hadn't imagined that attacking Yetunde would be so easy. The demented woman was blind to everything but Ebuka and a look of bewilderment entered her eyes as the solid head of the hammer smashed into her bulging midriff just below her ribs. She looked at Muna in disbelief, opened her mouth as if to say something, but only a thready sigh escaped as she staggered backwards, sucking desperately for air.

Muna pursued her, powering the hammer again and again into the same place. The solar plexus was Yetunde's favourite target when Muna annoyed her, and Muna always fell with the first punch, doubled up with pain and unable to breathe. Yetunde was too fat to succumb as quickly but Muna exulted in the wheezy puffs that issued from the bloated face as each blow landed. Every step the monstrous creature took brought her closer to the cellar door, and Muna fancied she heard the Devil laughing at the idea of having Yetunde for himself.

Yetunde tried to deflect the hammer with her hands, gasping out pleas to her husband. Ebuka! Ebuka! Help me! Help me!

But he didn't answer and Muna swung the hammer at Yetunde's kneecap, watching in fascination as pain caused her eyes to flare as wide as she had ever seen them. It was very satisfying.

The Master can't hear you, Princess. Your kicks have dazed him.

Yetunde held out her hands in a futile begging gesture. Let me be! I won't punish you if you stop now.

Muna ignored her and used guile of her own as she drove her weapon again at the woman's leg. You will suffer less if you enter the cellar yourself, Princess. I will not imprison you for long. When the Master has his strength back, I will release you.

Perhaps Yetunde's suffering was already too great for she grasped the doorjamb and stepped backwards on to the top step. Evil girl! she cried. You've hurt me badly!

Yes, Princess . . . and now you must go down the stairs of your own accord or the Devil will pull you down as easily as he pulled the Master.

Muna exulted at the fear she saw in Yetunde's face and wondered if the woman could hear the laughter from below. It was loud in Muna's ears. A deep guttural rumble that drew a hollow echo from the walls.

You're mad, Yetunde whispered.

I am what you've made me, Princess. All I know is what you've taught me.

She was gratified to see the same horror in Yetunde's face that had been in Ebuka's when she'd used similar words to him. It was strange. They had moulded Muna into mirrors of themselves yet they disliked their reflections.

I've been kind to you, Muna. I gave you a better home than you could ever have had in Africa.

Muna swung the hammer again. You gave me nothing, she said, using both hands to plunge the solid metal into Yetunde's mouth.

She stepped back, exhausted, as blood poured from the woman's lips, and she felt a marvellous thrill to hear the Devil's laugh rise from the caverns of the earth and see his hand reach out of the darkness to drag Yetunde down.

Ten

It seemed the Devil had made time stand still.

When Muna turned to look at Ebuka, he was still struggling to pull himself away from Yetunde's kicks, using his forearms and elbows to inch across the floor. Soundlessly, she replaced the hammer behind the photograph and then knelt to rock his shoulder. He gave a start of terror, wrapping his arms about his head and crying out to Yetunde to stop.

Princess isn't here, Master, she said.

Ebuka had used every ounce of his energy, dragging his paralysed legs behind him, and he was too tired to lift his face from the carpet or turn it towards her. Where is she? he asked.

I don't know, Master.

I heard her cry out.

Only at you, Master. She was shouting as she kicked you. I called to her to stop before she killed you . . . then ran to the sitting room to hide.

Are you sure she's not here?

Yes, Master. I believe she went upstairs. I heard the bedroom door slam before I came to see if you were all right. You must have heard it too. It was very loud.

I don't remember.

You're dazed, Master.

Ebuka dribbled on to the carpet. I think I lost consciousness. You must call the police. She's mad enough to kill us both.

I can't, Master. I don't know how.

He gave a groan of despair. Then what are we to do? Her mood will not have improved when she comes down again. Who will help us then?

What a weak and cowardly person he was, Muna thought. No one had helped her when Yetunde's rages had been ungovernable. Muna had taken a thousand more kicks and never once complained or begged for help.

I will bring the hoist to you, Master, and we will do what we practise each day. You must forget the pain Princess has caused you and find the strength to pull yourself into your chair. After that we will go outside as you planned. She will be calmer in an hour.

Ebuka showed more resolve once Muna wheeled the hoist into the hall, lowered the bar and helped him roll on to his back. He even managed to push himself into a sitting position when she told him she could hear Yetunde stamping around the bedroom. Fear persuaded him Muna was telling the truth, and with a massive heave he lifted himself far enough from the ground for Muna to slide the chair under his bottom.

He became helpless again when he was safely seated, like a little boy who'd done what was asked of him and refused to cooperate further. Muna dressed him in a waterproof jacket, brought a blanket for his legs and pushed him through the front door, tilting the chair backwards to ease it over the step on to the gravel drive. His weight was almost too much for her but necessity gave her strength. As each minute passed, she expected to hear Yetunde cry out.

You must stay here while I put on Abiola's boots and coat, Master. I will close this door so that Princess won't see you if she comes downstairs.

He looked alarmed. What if she attacks you?

She'll never catch me, Master. She's too fat. I will run as fast as I can if I see her on the stairs.

Muna listened outside the cellar door for several seconds before she pulled back the bolt and switched on the light. Princess lay on her back at the bottom of the steps, face bloodied and arms flung out. She was very dead. With a tiny sigh of relief, Muna plunged the cellar into darkness again and closed the door. Her sharp eyes picked out a tiny splatter of blood on the carpet at her feet, and she darted to the kitchen for a cloth. With great care she blotted the stain and searched for more. There were none. Yetunde had bled on the other side of the door but not on this.

Before she returned the cloth to the sink, she wiped the hammer clean, took Yetunde's Louis Vuitton handbag from the coffee table in the sitting room, checked it contained her wallet, make-up and mobile, then retrieved Yetunde's favourite Givenchy mackintosh from the cloakroom. With no time to select a better hiding place, she lifted the half-filled rubbish liner from the bin in the kitchen and placed everything she'd taken in the bottom, rearranging the liner on top.

Back in the hall, she pulled on Abiola's anorak and boots, put the front-door keys in her pocket and took a moment to calm her excitement and think. What else must she take to convince the Master that Yetunde had left the house while they were out? It was necessary for him to believe that or he would look for Yetunde inside, and Muna didn't want that. Her life had been better since Abiola disappeared. It would be better still if Yetunde did the same.

Ebuka frowned when Muna came out again. Why have you taken so long? What have you been doing?

Muna showed him Yetunde's mobile which she'd recovered from the bin, also the receiver from the landline in the sitting room. Collecting these, Master. It wouldn't be wise to let Princess call the police.

Why would she when she's at fault?

To make trouble for you, Master. She will say you struck her first and the white will believe her. The police already know you have a bad temper.

Ebuka gave a weary sigh, knowing Muna was right. What's this for? he asked as she laid the rod on his lap beside the handsets.

Protection against Princess for when we return, Master. You know now that you should carry it at all times. We'll be safer when she learns to fear you.

But Ebuka knew the only fear was in him. Yetunde's assault had frightened him badly, and he recognised that Muna had a greater understanding of her rages than he had. She wouldn't be preparing him to fight Yetunde otherwise.

He kept his thoughts to himself. Muna was sadly misguided if she thought he'd developed enough fondness for her to put her welfare before his own. In the choice between placating his bully of a wife with sugared almonds and credit cards, or taking the side of a powerless slave, he would placate Yetunde.

As he always had.

The cold December rain hurt Muna's cheeks and hands, and her feet slithered on the gravel as she tried to push the chair across it. It was hard work, even with Ebuka assisting her by turning the wheels, but she refused to listen to his pleas to sit in the summer house.

Princess will see us from her window, Master. She'll come after us and you'll have to threaten her with the rod sooner than you'd like.

Muna knew he would accept this argument for she had no illusions about him. He had been afraid of Yetunde's temper when he'd had the use of his legs. Now, hunched in misery at what had happened, he had even less desire to confront her. He kept rubbing the bruises on his arms and Muna was certain he was telling himself he couldn't go through such punishment again.

He seemed to read her thoughts. I'm not afraid of her, he said.

I think you are, Master, or you wouldn't have worked so hard to pull yourself into this chair.

At least I've proved I have the strength to do it.

Yes, Master. Princess will be surprised to find us gone when she comes down the stairs. It will worry her, I think.

Why?

She will know you're stronger and more courageous than she realised, Master. She said she didn't want you to go out but you've disobeyed her.

It was your idea, Muna.

No, Master. It was yours. The outside frightens me. Princess wouldn't have lost her temper if you hadn't ordered me to come.

What are you afraid of?

Everything, Master. My skin has never felt the rain or the cold. I like it better inside.

Have you never been out?

Never, Master. Princess says I'll die if I do. The whites have only hatred for piccaninnies. They'll kill me if I leave the house and become lost.

She's lying.

I don't think so, Master. They look unfriendly when I see them passing in the road or on the television.

She stopped his chair in front of the gate, took the rod and handsets from his lap and placed them in the lee of the wall. He asked her why she was doing it.

People will wonder why you're carrying them, Master. The rod is a fearsome weapon.

At least let me keep the mobile.

Muna crouched down to scoop leaf mould over the pile. Princess wouldn't like that, Master. She keeps her secrets in it.

All the more reason for me to look.

It won't make you happy, Master. It upset Princess to find pictures of white ladies in yours.

Perhaps Ebuka would have said more if a woman's shrill voice hadn't spoken from the other side of the gate. The sound was so unexpected – and so unwanted – that Muna shrank against the wall to avoid being seen.

'How nice to see you, Mr Songoli. Your wife led me to think you were too poorly to leave your bed but you look remarkably well. I must have misunderstood her.'

'I make a little progress each day, Mrs Hughes. This is the first time I've left the house since I came home.'

'Are you alone? Can I help you?' Muna heard the latch lift. 'At least let me ease you on to the pavement. My father always said gravel was the worst surface to cross.'

Ebuka gestured towards Muna. 'My daughter's with me.'

Muna peeped from beneath the anorak hood to see a witchy-looking white with long grey hair, broken veins in her cheeks and a hooked nose. Her fear intensified. The woman's eyes were as knowing as Inspector Jordan's.

Stop cowering away from her and stand up, Ebuka ordered sharply. You look ridiculous. She'll wonder what's wrong with you.

Muna rose to her feet but kept her gaze on the ground.

'How pretty she is. What's her name?'

'Muna.'

The woman reached out a hand to grip the girl's fingers in hers. 'I'm pleased to meet you, Muna.'

She's speaking to you, girl. Look at her.

Muna raised her head and felt the woman's eyes bore into her brain.

'I've spotted you at the windows, my dear, but never outside. I thought you'd be tall like your brothers. How deceptive distance is.'

Muna waited for Ebuka to say his daughter was brain-damaged and didn't understand English, but he stayed silent. Perhaps he was testing Muna. Perhaps he didn't believe her fear of strangers was genuine. What should she do? Speak? Or pull away and run back down the drive? She must speak, she thought. Ebuka could never be persuaded that Yetunde had left the house if they went back now.

Nervously, she ran her tongue across her lips. 'I watch you pass sometimes, lady,' she said. 'You live in the house next to this one, and you have three coats. A brown one, a blue one and a red one . . . but you like the red one best.'

Mrs Hughes arched her eyebrows in amusement. They were jet black and appeared to be drawn on her skin with a pen. Close to, she was old and ugly. 'How observant you are.'

Was that a good thing or a bad thing? Muna wondered. She wanted to remove her hand but the woman kept hold of it. There was warmth in the white fingers and their feel was unpleasant. The woman's *closeness* was unpleasant.

Mrs Hughes glanced at Ebuka. 'She's seems frightened of me. Is it my face? My grandchildren tell me I look like a witch.'

Ebuka was taken aback, but whether by the talkative white or his slave's ability to speak English, Muna didn't know. 'She has learning difficulties and it makes her timid,' he answered carefully. 'It's why she rarely leaves the house.'

'How old is she?'

'Fourteen.'

'She looks younger . . . and very different from her brothers. I wouldn't have known she was their sister if you hadn't told me.' Mrs Hughes placed her other palm on Muna's hand and rubbed it to give it some warmth. 'Her skin's icy-cold. Here' – she fished in her pocket and brought out some woollen gloves – 'have these. I've plenty more at home.'

Muna turned to Ebuka. What should I do, Master? If I take these things, she will come to the house looking for them . . . and Princess will be angry.

She's giving them as a gift. Smile and say thank you.

I'm frightened of her, Master. She sees all and knows all. She will ask more questions if we linger.

Do as I say and we can go.

Muna pushed up the corners of her mouth. 'Thank you, lady. Your gloves are pleasing to me . . . and so are you.'

Perhaps all whites could read other people's minds for Muna felt sure Mrs Hughes knew she was lying. 'I should have said sooner how sorry I am about your brother, my dear. It must have been a terrible shock for you.'

'Yes, lady.'

'But at least your father's getting better. You're obviously caring for him very well.'

'I make him do his exercises each day, lady.'

The woman pressed the gloves into Muna's hands and then glanced again at Ebuka. 'Will she manage the chair when you cross the roads? She's such a tiny little thing.'

'We're not going far.'

Mrs Hughes gave a troubled nod before saying her goodbyes and continued along the pavement.

Ebuka pointed in the same direction, indicating that they should follow her.

But Muna turned his chair the other way. No, Master, she said firmly. It's better to avoid Mrs Hughes. She knows I'm too thin to be the sister of Olubayo and Abiola. Princess would have fed me sugared almonds if I was truly her daughter.

Eleven

The world beyond the house was as threatening as Yetunde had promised. The overcast sky and unremitting rain turned everything grey, even the faces of passers-by, and Muna's heart lurched in alarm each time someone brushed against her or muttered in annoyance at having to step aside for Ebuka's chair. Dogs barked behind garden walls, car engines roared, cyclists splashed water into Muna's boots, and she was as wretched as she had ever been.

In her dreams of escape she had never pictured herself outside. Her rehearsed English words – 'Please help me. My name is Muna' – were always said to an imaginary white who came to the door when Yetunde was out. Yet Muna had never found the courage to put the plan into operation. If the bell rang when she was alone, she hid in a dark corner and held her breath until the stranger went away. It had been safer to obey Yetunde than risk placing trust in a white.

But now it was necessary to walk among them if she wanted to persuade Ebuka that Yetunde had left the house in anger while they were away, and great though her fear was, she tried to ignore it. Before long, however, she had lost her sense of direction and knew she wouldn't find her way home if Ebuka became impatient with her. She wasn't brave enough to ask a stranger where Twenty Three Fortis Row En Ten was.

Her slender arms ached from pushing the chair across paving stones. Her feet grew blisters inside Abiola's boots and her small reserves of energy were soon used up. She hadn't walked so far since Yetunde had stolen her. Tears of exhaustion limned her lashes but she kept her head down so that Ebuka wouldn't see them.

Everyone stared. First at the paralysed man and then at the ugly piccaninny behind him. Yetunde had been right to say they'd bring shame on themselves for Muna didn't think the smiles on the faces of the passers-by were kind. She found them mocking and cruel, and knew Yetunde had spoken the truth. A black should never expect help from a white.

Her courage deserted her completely when they came to a wide road, lined with shops and filled with vehicles and pedestrians. Ebuka pointed to some strange-looking lights and told her they could cross there, but Muna was too afraid to take another step. She came to a halt, her heart full of dread at the throng of blue-lipped, unsmiling people, hunched beneath umbrellas and jostling each other as cars and buses passed inches from their faces.

Her teeth chattered with cold. We must go back, Master.

But Ebuka's depression had lifted. Where Muna saw mockery in the faces that passed, he saw sympathy and consideration. We've barely gone half a mile, he said.

The house is small compared with this, Master. I've never been so far and your chair is hard to push. My legs are trembling.

Then rest.

Where, Master? If I squat here, people will ask what's wrong with me.

There's a café halfway down this road. My friends use it. We'll go there.

We can't do that, Master. They will wonder why I look so different from you and Princess. My skin is pale and the flesh on my bones is thin. It's better to say your daughter is too damaged to leave the house than parade her before people you know.

Ebuka conceded reluctantly, using his hands to turn the wheels as they made their way back. The effort made him irritable and he took out his ill humour on Muna, criticising her for hiding her face in her hood and dragging her feet along the ground.

You disappoint me, he growled. I thought you had more spirit.

I don't mean to, Master. I'm tired, that is all.

So am I, Muna, so am I . . . but you still expect me to protect you from Princess.

She will kill us both if you don't, Master.

You exaggerate.

I don't think so, Master. Princess wouldn't have told the witchy-white you were too sick to leave your bed if she doesn't intend you to die.

Any appetite Ebuka had ever had for confronting his wife was gone by the time they reached the gate. Before his accident, his habit had been to leave – walk out of the house and drive in search of the more congenial company of prostitutes – and then live with Yetunde's sulks until a new designer handbag appeared. It hadn't bothered him if she took out her anger on Muna or his sons as long as he didn't have to witness it.

He was less sanguine about being a victim himself, and demanded Muna give him Yetunde's smartphone so that he could call Jeremy Broadstone. Yetunde was too lazy to bother with passwords or codes so he'd find the solicitor's number easily enough. They'd wait on the pavement until he arrived. Princess never caused scenes in front of visitors.

Muna would have argued with him if she weren't afraid of raising his suspicions. He'd find her reluctance to accept the lawyer's protection strange when she'd warned so strongly that Yetunde was dangerous. But her heart sank at the idea of Mr Broadstone coming to the house. He thought like a policeman and would want to search it, and she had no explanation for what he would find. Her beautiful, vibrant dreams of hurting Yetunde hadn't taught her to deal with the consequences of inflicting pain. Only the joy of doing it.

She fetched the mobile and listened impassively to Ebuka's one-sided conversation with Mr Broadstone's secretary. Muna was better able to hide her fear of discovery than Ebuka was to hide his of Yetunde's anger. He became rude and belligerent when the secretary told him the lawyer was unavailable, accusing her of ignorance for not knowing that Mr Broadstone always took his calls.

Muna plucked at his sleeve when the line was cut abruptly. We should go inside, Master. Your neighbour is returning. She will wonder why we're on the pavement and ask more questions.

Had Ebuka turned round, he would have known Muna was lying, but he shook his head in frustration, persuaded that all women should be avoided. Muna took the mobile from his hand and dropped it into her pocket before lifting the latch on the gate.

The gravel is difficult, Master. You must turn the wheels as I push. I will take you to the summer house.

Ebuka grumbled loudly as the effort exhausted him further. Women were devils. They had no respect for men. They nagged and fought and disliked each other, whispering spiteful tittle-tattle to create division. Jealousy dominated all their relationships. It had been true of his mother and sisters when he was growing up, and it was true of Muna and her mistress.

Why should I believe you over Princess? he demanded irritably as Muna manoeuvred his chair through the summer-house door. You both talk nonsense. She accuses you of wanting to marry me and you accuse her of being a murderer. A man has to shut his ears to such idiocy if he wants control of his life.

Yes, Master.

Where are you going? he snapped as she turned back on to the grass.

To fetch the rod, Master. You will not have peace for long if Princess comes out.

Then leave me her smartphone. I'll call Inspector Jordan. Yetunde won't make trouble in front of her. She's afraid of her.

But Muna pretended not to hear. She slipped her feet from Abiola's boots and ran barefoot across the ice-cold grass. As she pulled the leaves from the rod, her tears returned and she belaboured herself for taking Yetunde's phone. All she'd wanted was a reason for why it hadn't been used but, instead, it had become the means by which Ebuka could summon the police.

The Devil was wrong to call her His Clever One.

Her thoughts were of punishment – worse than any she had yet experienced – as her senses left her and she slid quietly to the ground.

A hand caressed her cheek. 'Poor child. You're half-starved and your skin's icy-cold again. And so pale. Does your mother keep you out of the sun on purpose?' Muna recognised the voice of the witchy-white. A finger touched the raised scar on her foot. 'I think you can hear me, Muna. Why are you without shoes or socks? And what's this? Did someone burn you deliberately? Talk to me, child. Why are you out here alone? Where's your father?'

Muna knew she had to speak but she was tired and her thoughts were chaotic. She told the truth because it was all she could remember but she hadn't the energy to open her eyes. 'He's in the summer house, lady. I came to fetch the rod and the telephone. I had to run fast so I took off Abiola's boots. Am I sick?'

'No, dear, you just asked too much of yourself. There's not enough of you to do anything strenuous. I was passing the gate as you came towards it and saw you drop a few seconds later.' An arm slipped beneath Muna's neck and helped her sit up. 'Lean forward. You'll feel better soon.'

After that, Muna didn't have to do or say anything. Mrs Hughes lifted her in her arms and took her to Ebuka, demanding explanations. She wanted to know why a fourteen-year-old was so undernourished that a woman could carry her easily. She wanted to know why Muna never left the house, why she was wearing boots that were too big for her, why her foot had burn scars on it, and why a rod and a telephone handset had been left beside the gate.

'I've been a teacher all my life, Mr Songoli, and I can recognise abuse when I see it. Are you aware that using excessive force against a child is illegal in this country? It disturbed me greatly to see that rod.'

But Ebuka wanted none of it. 'You must talk to my wife,' he said, lowering his head into his hands. 'I'm weary of making excuses for her.'

Mrs Hughes sat Muna on a chair. 'What does he mean?'

Muna's mind cleared as her strength came back. 'Mamma has a temper,' she answered timidly. 'It's become worse since we lost Abiola. She takes out her distress on all of us. We brought the rod outside to protect ourselves in case she came after us.' She leaned forward to ease back the sleeve of Ebuka's jacket. 'She made these marks on Dada's arms this morning by pulling him from his chair and kicking him. He tried to defend himself but the blows to his head dazed him.'

The deep discoloration on the dark skin was obvious and Mrs Hughes looked shocked. 'Did you call the police?'

'No, lady. They can't mend Mamma's sadness. We came outside to get away from her. She'll be calmer now.'

'Indeed . . . but—' Mrs Hughes broke off to take Muna's hand. 'Does she hurt *you*, child? Does she feed you less than your brothers? Did she cause that burn on your foot?'

'No, lady. I dropped hot oil through clumsiness when I was young, and there are things wrong with my brain, which is why I find it hard to eat. Olubayo's brain is damaged also. He became epileptic with the stress of Abiola's departure. Mamma is very upset about it. She's ashamed to have feeble-minded children and a husband who can't walk.'

Mrs Hughes looked uncomfortable as if Muna had said more than she should. 'Is this true, Mr Songoli? Your son has epilepsy?'

He nodded. 'We lurch from one tragedy to another. Yetunde finds it hard to cope.'

'Then she needs help. We have excellent social services in this borough. At the very least let me help you organise some respite care.'

Muna spoke before Ebuka could. 'What is respite, lady?'

'Relief . . . support. Nurses will come in to look after your father so that your mother can have some time to herself. Would she like that, do you think?'

Muna decided Mrs Hughes wasn't as knowing as she'd first thought. She looked stupid with her pencilled eyebrows arched in eager enquiry. 'I'm sure she would, lady,' she said, lifting her lips into a shy smile. 'Will you speak to her about it? She will listen more to you than to me or Dada. If you help me push him into the house, it will give you a reason to talk with her. Her anger should be gone by now.'

'Is that what you want me to do?'

'It is, lady.' Muna drew the front-door keys from her anorak pocket and gave them to the woman. 'I brought these in case she refused to let us in.'

Muna hung back when they reached the entrance so it was Mrs Hughes who unlocked the door and tilted Ebuka's chair over the threshold. The rod lay across his knees and he clutched at it fearfully as the woman eased him into the hall. He called Yetunde's name several times but his shouts were greeted with silence. Even Muna, hypersensitive to sounds from the cellar, heard nothing.

Mrs Hughes steered the chair towards the sitting room and peered inside. 'I wonder where she's gone.'

'She went upstairs just before Muna and I left,' Ebuka told her. 'We heard her slam the bedroom door.'

'Would you like me to look?'

'I think Muna should go.'

But Muna shook her head and spoke in Hausa. I'm too frightened, Master. Princess might hit me.

It seemed Mrs Hughes didn't need a translation. Whatever she saw in Muna's face, or heard in her tremulous tones, persuaded her to ignore Ebuka. Muna thought her brave as she mounted the stairs since she couldn't know what was up there. Perhaps her courage came from being white.

She waited until Mrs Hughes's footsteps sounded on the landing and then touched Ebuka's shoulder, pointing to the coffee table in the sitting room. Princess's handbag has gone, Master. It was there when I took her mobile. Shall I see if her coat is missing?

Twelve

Yetunde was a sorry sight. She sat with her back propped against the far wall, her fat legs splayed in front of her, her dress bunched in ugly folds around her midriff and a pool of urine between her thighs. The dust of the floor was in her hair and on her skin, and tears of anguish had smudged her mascara. Her lips, swollen to twice their size and caked with dried blood, gave her the look of a clown, and, try as she might, she could not prise them open.

Muna squatted at a distance, looking to see what else was wrong with the woman. The scuff marks and bloodstains on the stones showed where she'd crawled to her position by the wall, but the way her hands lay in her lap, pink palms uppermost, looked unnatural.

I thought you were dead, Princess. I'd have been frightened to let Mrs Hughes into the house if I'd known you weren't.

She tapped the end of the rod on the puffy swelling of the woman's knee where the hammer had smashed the kneecap; then she manoeuvred it under Yetunde's right wrist and studied the end of the white bone that protruded from the skin. Agony sent quivers of shock through the woman's gigantic body but no sound emerged from the scabbed lips, just throaty grunts that were expelled with mucus from her nose.

Satisfied that Yetunde couldn't hurt her, Muna inched forward to place the Louis Vuitton handbag and Givenchy mackintosh on her lap. She had been busy in the three hours since Mrs Hughes left, even remembering to slip Yetunde's mobile into Ebuka's pocket.

The witchy-white has gone and the Master fell asleep soon afterwards, Princess. He is worn out by your attack on him and the distance we travelled. Both are persuaded you've gone shopping. The Master said it's what you always do when you're angry – spend money on yourself. The witchy-white believed him. She says you have more shoes and coats than anyone she's ever seen.

She watched Yetunde try to lift one of her hands to open the handbag.

There's no rescue in there, Princess. I took your mobile when the Master and I went out. I'm much cleverer than you think I am. I remembered Inspector Jordan saying that such phones can tell the police everything, even where a person is when they're using it . . . and I knew they'd find it strange if you didn't use it while you were shopping. It's better that the Master keeps it from now on. He'll show it to the police, and they'll learn as little from it as they did from Abiola's.

She tilted her head to one side to stare intently into Yetunde's face.

You're very ugly, Princess. You'll shame us all if anyone finds you like this. You have the face and voice of a pig, and you smell from the fluids that are leaking out of you. People will say the Master was right to prefer his little piccaninny when they discover how dirty and ugly you are. They will see he married a sow and not a wife. Do you wish now you'd been kinder to little Muna?

As always, she found it easy to read Yetunde's thoughts. Yetunde never disguised her feelings. She believed it made her powerful when her anger inspired fear and her forgiveness brought relief. Muna watched the popping eyes swing between rage and panic – blazing one minute, pleading the next – but she saw that Yetunde's primary emotion was despair.

She was in the same friendless place that Ebuka had been, with the same shocked understanding that the girl who crouched before her was a stranger. The furthest her imagination had ever taken her was to accuse Muna of having demons; she'd never thought that a child, so silent and obedient for so many years, might want to kill her.

I think you hope that Olubayo will look for you when he comes home, Princess, but he won't. He seeks relief from your vicious tongue as much as the Master does, and will believe what his father tells him . . . that you had a tantrum and have gone away to sulk.

Yetunde shook her head.

You mustn't wish for things that won't happen, Princess. When you don't come home tonight, Olubayo and I will search your room and we'll find that your most expensive clothes are missing . . . along with this bright blue suitcase and everything you need to make yourself pretty.

She gestured to the case that stood beside her.

When the Master fell asleep, I packed it with your nicest dresses, your best perfumes and most precious jewellery. Olubayo will find it all gone . . . and when he tells the Master, the Master will think you've taken yourself to a hotel . . . as you did when you found the pictures of white ladies on his telephone. You spent his money for five days to teach him a lesson about squandering it on whores.

Muna opened the Louis Vuitton handbag and took out Yetunde's passport.

Then the Master will look for this in the drawer of the sideboard, and discover it missing also. It's good that you lost your temper with him today because you made him hate and fear you. He'll believe you've gone to your sister in Africa – as you always tell him you will when you're angry – and he'll be glad. He'll find joy again without you.

Yetunde closed her eyes. Fresh tears oozed through the mascara.

Ebuka was awake when Muna returned to his bedroom. She helped him into his wheelchair and pushed him to the sitting room, saying he should watch the programmes he enjoyed for as long as he wanted. Yetunde would demand to see something different when she returned, but he must stay firm. She will respect you more if you do, Master.

He rubbed a weary hand around his face. Things have gone too far, Muna. I've been going through her mobile, and you're right that she wants me dead. She's written vile texts to her sister, saying it's a pity I didn't die.

She used the same words to Mr Broadstone, Master.

We shouldn't be in the same house. It's not healthy for either of us. I'm not keen to be here when she comes back.

Olubayo will be home soon, Master. You'll feel safer when he is. Princess won't attack you both.

Muna listened from the kitchen as Ebuka recounted the events of the morning to his son. The tale he told was dramatic. Yetunde had gone mad, almost killing her husband with the ferocity of her onslaught. Ebuka had managed to save himself by using the hoist to get back into the chair but there was no knowing what would have happened if he and Muna hadn't fled the house.

Olubayo – flattered to have his father confide in him – urged Ebuka to call the police before Mamma came home. It would take more than a day of shopping to cool her anger. When Ebuka appeared to agree with him, Muna took them bowls of broth on a tray. Olubayo glared at her, seeing the intrusion for what it was – a way to attract Ebuka's attention to herself – but she pretended not to notice. Instead she made a point of praising him.

You look happier, Master. I said your son would be a comfort to you. He won't let harm come to you. He is stronger and more determined than his mother knows.

He wants me to call the police.

Muna stooped to put the tray on the coffee table. Perhaps he's right, Master. Mrs Hughes thought the same. She seemed very shocked that Princess had hurt you so badly. The Inspector will ask many questions about why Princess lost her temper . . . and some might be hard to answer . . . but she'll know you have reason to fear your wife when you show her your bruises.

Olubayo didn't like Muna giving her views. The Inspector won't come, he said scornfully. It'll be a man in a car who'll tell Dada to keep the door locked and call again when Mamma returns.

He'll know that Abiola's still missing.

What if he does?

He will tell Inspector Jordan that Princess caused her husband damage, and she will come here to find out why. She believes the Master lost his temper with Abiola. It will interest her to learn that Princess's anger is worse.

Ebuka told them to stop arguing and ate his broth in silence. When he'd finished, he ordered Muna to bolt the front door. There would be time enough to decide what to do when Yetunde returned. They would know what mood she was in as soon as she discovered she was locked out.

Muna listened outside Olubayo's door for several minutes before she eased it open to make sure he was asleep. She had no need of a light. Years of confinement had trained her to interpret every shadow in the darkness, and she could see Olubayo quite clearly. He lay curled on his side, his lids fast closed, his breathing deep and regular.

She slipped silently down the stairs to check on Ebuka and found him as dead to the world as his son, his snores reaching her even before she opened the dining-room door. It was good that his doctors had given him pills to send him to sleep. She knew them by the colour of the packet, and it had been easy to crush two into his night-time drink and one into Olubayo's.

Poor Yetunde. Even if she were able to call for help, no one but Muna would hear her.

Muna placed a lit candle on the cellar floor and crouched beside it, seeing with satisfaction that Princess's eyes were open. Cold, fear and pain were keeping her awake for the brain and the body couldn't rest when these three evils existed together. Muna understood this and exulted that Princess had learned it also. It was right and just that she should suffer as Muna had.

Her position had barely altered since Muna had wrapped parcel tape across her mouth and secured her fractured wrists to the handles of two heavy trunks. Only her uninjured leg had shifted slightly, as if to relieve pressure on a nerve or a muscle. Perhaps the agony of movement was too great or the shallowness of her breath had robbed her of energy. Every inhale and exhale was through her nose, and each was constricted by the mucus her grunts had caused.

How frightened she looked, Muna thought. Had she prayed and prayed that someone who cared for her would come down the steps? Or had she heard the Devil's laughter in the walls? Muna could hear it and feel it. A deep rumble that set the air of the cellar trembling and vibrating.

She watched Yetunde patiently for several minutes, and would have watched longer if she hadn't felt the need for sleep herself. The day had been tiring and she still had much to do. But it gave her pleasure to see terror in Yetunde's wide rolling eyes. She placed her hand on the packed suitcase that she'd left beside Yetunde that afternoon.

All hope is lost to you, Princess. Olubayo has searched your room and discovered this gone, and the Master has looked in the sideboard and knows your passport is missing. They believe you've left in a rage to visit your sister so the police will not be called . . . and that pleases the Master because he doesn't want whites to know how little his wife respects him.

She peered curiously into Yetunde's bulging, pleading eyes, and then rose to her feet and began moving the boxes and trunks that were piled against the back wall. Behind them were a series of ancient floor-to-ceiling iron racks, dirty with dust and cobwebs. Some of the slots contained empty wine bottles but most were unfilled. In places, Muna could see where hands had rested on the metal, disturbing the dust, and she wondered if the prints had been made by Ebuka when he removed her mattress, or the police when they searched the cellar for Abiola.

She was careful to leave no marks as she slid her hand through a slot at waist level and used her fingertips to locate the crevice in the thin stone veneer behind it. At first, since it never occurred to her that Yetunde and Ebuka were ignorant of the cellar's second chamber, her reluctance to touch any part of the iron frame had been through fear of being punished if Yetunde realised she'd discovered it. But as time went by, and she saw that the Songolis were unaware of it, her desire grew to keep the knowledge from them.

The secret belonged to Muna and no one else. The Devil had revealed it to her one night when Ebuka had left his torch on the floor beside her mattress. She didn't know how long she'd been in the house – *A week? A season? A year?* – but when she found the courage to switch on the beam, the cellar became less frightening. Until then it had been steeped in ominous shadow, glimpsed only in the backwash of light from the hall when Yetunde held the door open to allow her in at night or out again in the morning.

By torchlight it was smaller than her imagination had made it – half the size of the hall and cloakroom under which it stood – and her attention was drawn immediately to the dusty honeycomb of metal in front of her because the beam of the torch was shining straight at it. She thought it a strange way to build shelves until she saw bottles in some of the slots and guessed what its purpose was. There was nothing else apart from a card that glowed white against the blackness of the iron rack.

It hung by a string from the neck of an empty bottle and Muna could make out the picture even from five yards away. It was simple and clear – the outline of a hand with the long middle finger extended – and she would believe for ever that it had been put there for her to find. Where others might have dismissed the diagram as an obscene joke, Muna took it for a sign and followed the instruction exactly, removing the bottle and sliding her arm into the slot.

She turned to look at Yetunde now as her finger pressed on the latch inside the crevice and a section of the wall detached itself from the rest. She used her toe against the sturdy bar at the bottom of the metal to push it wider, and gloried to see the absolute terror in Yetunde's face as a new level of cold crept towards her.

On the floor inside the second room lay the picture of the pointing finger. Muna had placed it there to prevent Yetunde discovering the secret, but, as the stale air stirred with the opening of the door, the card flipped over to show the writing on the reverse. Without the ability to decipher what it said, Muna believed the Devil had written it. And what more proof did she need than his rumbling laugh as the card lifted and turned?

This walk-in safe was designed and constructed in 1983 by Joseph Baumgarten. The patented concealed door is a strengthened aluminium alloy frame with a natural stone veneer, operated by cantilever hinges, counter-weights and a finger latch. For optimum performance, maintenance should include regular oiling of these mechanisms. The manufacturer guarantees all moving parts for ten years but takes no liability for breaches of security through carelessness or indiscretion. There is no lock. The strength of a concealed safe relies on silence.

She retrieved the hammer from where she'd placed it on the bottom step. You must enter of your own accord, Princess. If you do not, I will use this until you do.

Yetunde shook her head.

Then you will suffer agony, Princess. And even if the tape and the scabs burst on your mouth, and screams escape you, the Master and Olubayo won't hear them. Their sleep isn't natural. It comes from pills and not from tiredness.

She split the tie that held Yetunde's right wrist and watched the hand drop with a thud to the floor before placing the metal head of the hammer on the protruding bone and rocking it from side to side. Groans and grunts reverberated in Yetunde's throat.

I'd like you to scream, Princess. I go to sleep each night wanting to hear you beg. My dreams are happy ones – full of blood – and I feel better when I wake. Do you want to die, Princess?

She split the tie holding the other wrist then lifted the hammer as if to strike, but Yetunde had already begun the painful process of shuffling her obese body towards the open door of the second chamber.

Thirteen

Barely a day passed before Ebuka grew unsettled about Yetunde's departure. Muna blamed the witchy-looking neighbour who rang the doorbell on the second morning. She invited herself inside and looked at Ebuka in surprise when he said he hadn't heard from Yetunde. He explained that his wife had taken her clothes, suitcase and passport, and he assumed she planned to stay away for some time. After that, Mrs Hughes became inquisitive.

Was it normal for Mrs Songoli to go away without warning? Had she done such a thing before? And how had she managed to leave so quickly? There had been less than an hour between Mrs Hughes speaking with Ebuka at the gate and her finding Muna in a faint. Had either of them seen a taxi pass? At the very least Mr Songoli should call Yetunde's friends to discover if they knew where she was. What if she'd met with an accident?

Ebuka's resentment at being interrogated by a virtual stranger meant his answers were curt, and Muna saw that Mrs Hughes found them suspicious. She stepped in to make the explanations herself. Mamma always threatened to leave when she was angry . . . She kept her suitcase in her bedroom cupboard for that reason . . . They had seen many taxis while they were out but hadn't thought to look for her in them . . . It was a good idea to speak with her friends . . . She would persuade her father to make the calls after Mrs Hughes left.

Mrs Hughes appeared to accept what she said but Muna noticed that her curious eyes were never still. Every so often she glanced towards the stairs, tilting her head as if listening for sounds. 'It's unkind to put you through the same trauma you suffered at the time Abiola was taken,' she murmured. 'I wonder why she'd want to keep any of you guessing about where she is.'

'I think Mamma might want to punish Dada in this way, lady,' Muna whispered shyly. 'It upset her very much when he told me to put on Abiola's anorak and boots so that I could take him outside. I said I didn't want to, but Dada insisted and that's what made her angry. I think she feels he doesn't remember Abiola often enough.'

Perhaps Ebuka knew this was true for he gave a tired shrug of recognition. 'I don't think about him as much as I should. Days go by and his name's never mentioned. I should have realised how his loss must have impacted on Yetunde, but all my energy has gone into coping with this wretched disability.' He smacked his useless legs. 'I've been inconsiderate.'

Mrs Hughes walked to the door of the sitting room and ran a thoughtful gaze around it. 'She can't have called a taxi on that phone,' she said, nodding towards the landline. 'Muna had the handset in the garden. I wondered why at the time.'

'I took it to stop her breaking it after Dada threatened to call the police, lady. Mamma destroys things when she's angry. She hopes it will show Dada how upset she is.'

'Is that why she's happy to leave him wondering where she's gone?'

Muna nodded. 'She says he'll look for her if he loves her. I'll help him do that now. Together we will make the calls to Mamma's friends.'

Unexpectedly, the woman raised her hand to the girl's cheek and stroked it gently. 'She's wrong to leave you with so much responsibility, Muna. You're too young for it.'

'I like caring for Dada, lady, and I know all that has to be done.' She opened the front door. 'Mamma will come back soon and I will tell her how kind you've been. She will like you as a friend, I think.'

Ebuka was harder to pacify. Once the seed of doubt was planted in his mind, it grew and multiplied. How *had* Yetunde left so quickly? They both knew she couldn't have called a taxi since Muna had taken her mobile as well as the landline. Which left what? That Princess had walked away, dragging her suitcase behind her? Impossible. Yetunde never walked anywhere. And why hadn't *he* seen the similarity between his wife's and his son's disappearance? What were the chances of two members of one family vanishing into thin air within months of each other unless the same person took both?

Muna brought him Yetunde's mobile, which he'd left on charge in his bedroom. I don't know, Master, but the numbers of Princess's friends will be in here. I think you should do as the white suggested and call them. I believe she was waiting for a friend when she lost her temper with you.

What gives you that idea?

She was in her best dress and using her most expensive handbag, Master. She never did that unless she was going out.

Ebuka frowned, trying to recall what Yetunde was wearing, but Muna knew that, even if he remembered, he wouldn't be able to say if it was Princess's 'best'.

What are you suggesting? That she planned to leave the house anyway . . . and her friend just happened to turn up during the time we were absent?

I don't know, Master. I can only tell you what I saw.

Ebuka eyed her with distrust. You're very quick with your answers. Are any of them true? You lied to Mrs Hughes about Yetunde saying she'd break the handset if I called the police.

Muna turned away. You were dazed, Master. Princess said many things you didn't hear.

Where are you going?

To the kitchen, Master. You're unkind to be angry with me. It's not my fault if someone took Princess away.

She closed the door to shut him out but placed her ear against the panels to listen to the handful of calls he made. He was too ashamed to say his wife had left him after an argument, and asked only if Yetunde was there. Each time he was told she wasn't, followed by curious questions about why he thought she might be. As the conversations became increasingly awkward, he gave up and wheeled himself into the sitting room.

Shortly afterwards Muna heard the television playing, and she thought how clever she'd been to urge him to talk to Yetunde's friends. He would hesitate to try again. He disliked women too much to give them a reason to laugh at him.

Muna never imagined she might regret being rid of Yetunde. In truth she hadn't believed it was possible to make a woman so huge and gross vanish so easily. If she'd pictured a future at all it was that life would be pleasanter when Princess learned to fear her.

Only now that Yetunde was absent did Muna understand how necessary she was. Problems arose that Muna hadn't foreseen and couldn't solve. She'd thought Yetunde lazy but it seemed she'd done more than Muna realised.

The cupboards and fridge were almost empty of food. There was no detergent to wash clothes and sheets, no replacement disposable gloves to handle Ebuka's catheter and prevent infection, no fluid to clean and sterilise the bags. And Muna was ignorant of how to acquire these things. Nothing had ever run out while Yetunde was there. Goods had arrived each week though Muna didn't know how Yetunde ordered or paid for them. Nor had she seen who delivered them. If she was downstairs, she was sent to the kitchen; if she was upstairs, all she saw from the windows was the roof and sides of a white van.

Everything was left in the hall, packed in plastic bags with red and blue letters. These told Muna nothing since she was unable to decipher them, but she guessed they spelled the name of a shop. Before Abiola went missing, this wasn't important. As long as the plastic bags arrived, she was able to make the meals Yetunde demanded; without them, she could do nothing.

She remembered her terror when she opened the cupboards on the day the police left and discovered them bare. Yetunde's temper would be bad enough when she returned from the hospital with Olubayo to find Ebuka dead in the cellar, but she would be beside herself if Muna told her there was nothing to eat. Princess's rages were always worse when she was hungry.

For once, Muna's fears hadn't materialised. It seemed to have something to do with the new mobile Yetunde had bought on her way home by taxi. She was certainly more interested in that than she was in Ebuka, refusing to accompany him to the hospital because she couldn't leave her newly diagnosed epileptic son. She stood at the door until the ambulance had gone; then, free of watchers, she settled herself in a comfortable chair and gave all her attention to her new toy. A few hours later plastic bags appeared in the hall again.

Muna asked Olubayo how it was possible to purchase food by tapping a tiny screen but he said she was too stupid to understand. She couldn't read or write or recognise numbers. Think of it as magic, he told her.

She didn't ask again. It wasn't wise to let Olubayo believe himself superior. With his father absent and his mother only interested in Jeremy Broadstone, he'd turned his attention back to Muna. She couldn't count the number of times she'd looked up to find him staring at her with desire in his eyes. When she hid her weapons about the house, they were as much to defend herself against Olubayo as against Yetunde.

But ignorance didn't help her now. Ebuka knew nothing about food and its preparation. He'd said many times that it was the woman's place to cook and clean, so she doubted he had the will or the patience to listen while she listed the items she wanted, or that he knew how and where to buy them if she could persuade him to make such a list. In any case, she didn't want to remind him of Princess's importance. He might strive harder to find her.

Mrs Hughes was surprised to find Muna on her doorstep. She took the girl's hand and drew her inside, admonishing her for coming out in a thin dress and fabric shoes. 'Does your father know you're here?' she asked, leading her into a sitting room.

'No, lady. I didn't want him to worry. I waited until he fell asleep in front of the television.'

She stared about the room, marvelling at how different it was from the one she knew. Yetunde's was white and clean and looked like the pictures in the magazines on the coffee table. Mrs Hughes's was cluttered and dirty. The sofa and chairs were old and faded, a threadbare carpet covered the floor and paintings were hung on every inch of the dark blue walls. She wondered if all whites lived in squalor.

Mrs Hughes smiled at her expression. 'Don't you like pictures, Muna?'

'I'm not sure, lady. There are none in our house.'

'I saw a photograph of your mother in the hall.'

'It's the only one, lady. The others are in a book that Mamma keeps in a drawer.'

She'd found the courage to look through the album early on when Yetunde was out. If Yetunde was truly her aunt then there might be pictures of her mother, even herself as a baby. But she was disappointed. Every woman's face looked like Yetunde's and none like hers.

Mrs Hughes gestured towards a chair. 'Sit down and tell me how I can help you. Let's start with why you think it would worry your father if he knew you were here.'

Muna perched on the edge of the seat. 'He wouldn't want me to tell you we have no food, lady. He's ashamed that Mamma left . . . but more ashamed that he doesn't know how to make the white van come to the house.'

'Which white van?'

'I don't know, lady.' She spread a plastic bag across her knees. 'This is what the food comes in. I think the red and blue letters spell the name of a shop.'

'It's a supermarket chain. Your mother must have ordered what she wanted online.'

Muna took Yetunde's smartphone from her pocket. 'She used this, lady. All I need is for you to show me what she did so that I can teach Dada.'

She watched Mrs Hughes closely to see if she found it strange that Muna had Yetunde's mobile. She'd taken it from Ebuka's lap while he dozed, heart in mouth as she tiptoed towards the front door. There was much to fear – the Master's questions if he found her missing; this white's questions about why Princess had left her smartphone in the house – but her desire to learn and gain Yetunde's power was greater.

If Mrs Hughes was curious, she didn't show it, commenting only that she was surprised Mrs Songoli didn't use a security code. She invited Muna to sit on the sofa beside her, held the girl's forefinger in hers and took her through the process of turning on the smartphone, recognising the icons in the menu and flicking the screen to the one she wanted. Muna selected the app that looked like the markings on the plastic bag.

'What now, lady?'

'You need your mother's password.'

'What's that, lady?'

'A series of letters or numbers. Some people use their birthdays because they're easy to remember.'

'I know when Mamma's is, lady. It happens each time the year comes to an end. She watches fireworks on the television and says they're for her.'

'The thirty-first of December.'

'I expect so, lady.'

'How old is she?'

'The great four-oh. I don't know what it means but she doesn't like it.'

Mrs Hughes smiled. 'It means she was born forty years ago last December . . . which would make her birth date thirty-one twelve nineteen seventy-three. Would you like me to try that or would you rather ask your father when you go home? We only have three guesses.'

'Dada won't know, lady. I want you to try.'

Muna saw unease in Mrs Hughes's face as the password was accepted, and guessed she'd only agreed to help because she hadn't expected it to work. Nevertheless, she showed Muna how to discover what Yetunde had ordered before, how to fill the shopping basket, select a delivery time and go to checkout. Her patience even extended to clearing the screen and inviting the girl to repeat the steps on her own.

Her unease deepened as Muna's agile finger took her unerringly through the steps and selected the correct digits for the password once she entered the app. 'You know your numbers?'

'No, lady. I remembered which order you pressed the squares.'

'That's quite a talent, Muna. I'm surprised your mother didn't teach you to do this.'

Muna slowed her finger. 'She tried, lady, but I made mistakes and she grew impatient. Watching you has helped me remember what she did.'

'Has she ever given you lessons in reading?'

'When I was younger, lady. But they were hard and I couldn't do them. The doctors say it's because my brain is damaged.'

Mrs Hughes let a silence develop as Muna found her way to 'checkout' and looked up with a gleam of triumph in her eyes. 'Well done. Now all your father has to do is agree that the order is correct and enter his credit-card details.'

'He won't know how to do that, lady. He never orders things this way. He says it's a woman's place to buy what her husband needs.'

Mrs Hughes studied her for a moment. 'Is he angry with you because there's no food in the house?'

'No, lady. He doesn't know. I haven't told him.'

'Why not?'

'Because there's nothing he can do to fill the shelves and it upsets me to see him cry. He's been sad since his accident. Mamma tells him over and over again that he's not a man any more . . . and he believes it.'

Mrs Hughes reached for a wallet which lay on the seat of the armchair next to her. She flipped it open and removed a small piece of plastic. 'I'll show you what you have to do, Muna, but in return I want you to be honest with me.'

'What about, lady?'

'Why you and your father say you have brain damage when you clearly don't. You can work out your answer while I show you which of these numbers must go in the box.' She ran Muna's finger along the embossed figures on the front. 'These are the ones you need. You must look for them on the keypad. You may not know their names but you'll be able to find them by their shape.'

She waited while Muna copied each of the sixteen digits into the phone; then she took it back from her and deleted them again. 'When you use your father's card, be sure to copy each shape accurately or it won't work. Do you understand? I'll be very unhappy if you've memorised my number.'

Muna tucked the mobile back into her pocket. 'I haven't, lady. Now I must go back to Dada.'

'You didn't answer my question.'

'The truth is what Dada and I have told you, lady, but you don't believe it. Would you like me to invent a different story to make you happy?'

A look of amusement crossed Mrs Hughes's face. 'I'm sure you'd come up with a good one.' She took the bag that Muna had brought. 'At least let me give you some food to see you through today. I have some of the items your mother likes in my fridge.'

'I can't pay you, lady.'

'I don't expect you to. Think of it as a gift from a friend.' She rose to her feet and looked down at the girl. 'You need a friend, don't you, Muna?'

Muna ducked her head in pretended gratitude, but her heart fluttered nervously. Her first impression of Mrs Hughes had been right. This witchy-white was as knowing and clever as she was.

Fourteen

Ebuka's ill-humour of the morning had passed, helped by the fried chicken, spiced rice and beans that Muna gave him for lunch. It was always his favourite, reminding him of meals his mother had made. He still harboured doubts about the speed of Yetunde's departure, but since he couldn't see anyone taking her against her will – her bulk alone would have prevented it – he decided Muna's suggestion was correct.

I can just imagine Princess storming out of the house with an acquaintance and demanding to be dropped at a hotel. If she isn't home by tomorrow, I'll contact the credit-card company to find out where she's staying.

Muna was putting him through his exercises, crooking his left knee over her arm and manipulating his foot. How will they know, Master?

Her card will tell them. She can't book into a hotel without one.

What else does a card do, Master? Is it like a smartphone and the cameras in the roads that take photographs? Can it find a person?

Only if they're staying in a hotel. Otherwise it shows where they've been shopping. If I discover Princess is costing me a fortune, I'll cancel it. She'll come back soon enough when she's deprived of funds.

Perhaps she's not using the card because she doesn't want you to know where she is, Master. What will you do then?

Call the police, said Ebuka, using the hoist to pull himself into a sitting position. It'll mean something's happened to her.

Muna shone the torch beam into Yetunde's face and this time there was no question the woman was dead. Her head was tilted back against the wall as if she were stretching her neck in a last attempt to breathe, but her half-open eyes were glazed and milky. There was no air in the second chamber when the door was closed. Muna knew this from shutting herself inside in the early days. The idea of starving to death hadn't troubled her – Yetunde gave her so little to eat anyway – but her panicky struggle for breath as she slowly asphyxiated had persuaded her she'd rather live.

She moved the beam to pick out Abiola where he lay on the floor. She'd shown Yetunde her son before she plunged her into darkness by sealing the door. It pleased her to think Yetunde had died knowing that Muna was cleverer than the police. Had she cried for Abiola or only for herself?

The fat, ugly boy seemed quite unchanged. Muna thought he'd be a skeleton by now, his bones as white as the animal bones she remembered from her childhood. Dogs and cats lay scattered about the road outside the schoolyard, knocked down by cars before birds picked them clean. She thought all death was the same.

Yet Abiola was still clothed in his school uniform and his face was pleasant to look at. In truth Muna found him more attractive in death than she had in life. He was thinner and more handsome. Like the unspoilt four-year-old he'd been before Yetunde taught him that Muna could be beaten and kicked for every little mistake she made. There was a time – quite brief – when Muna had wanted to love Abiola, for she'd yearned to show and receive affection, but he'd learned all too quickly that she was a person of no account and treated her with the same cruelty as his mother.

Yetunde had found his antics amusing until he turned his temper tantrums on her. By then it was too late. Abiola had become unmanageable, and the only way to pacify him was with sweets and treats. Such things made him worse. The fatter he grew the more monstrous and demanding he became, delighting in the pain he caused with his fleshy fists and heavy feet.

How Muna had loathed him, having to take the punishment when he stole food and being forced to clean the filth from his sheets and underwear every day. It had pleased her to lure him into this chamber and leave him to die. The Devil had laughed as the door closed and his cries of rage and fear were muffled.

It was his own fault. Had he gone to school as he should, it would not have happened. Instead he crept back into the house after his mother left, and Muna found him eating the creamy chocolate dessert that Yetunde had ordered for the meal that evening, digging his fingers into the soft mixture and stuffing it into his mouth.

I'll tell Mamma *you* ate it, he said. You know she'll believe me.

She won't like it that you haven't gone to school on the day she's away, Muna answered, placing his soiled bedding on the floor beside the washing machine.

I'll tell her I felt sick. He dropped the bowl in the sink and opened the cupboards. Where are the salt and vinegar crisps? I'll beat you if you don't tell me. I know you hide them so you won't get punished when there aren't enough for Mamma.

Muna watched his chocolate-covered fingers leave a smear of sticky grime on the handles, and she thought of the time and effort it would take to clean them before Yetunde came home.

She lowered her gaze in pretended fear and spoke in a tearful whisper. I keep them in the cellar, Master. There's a cupboard no one knows about except me. I hide your favourite food in there so you can't steal it and get me into trouble.

What a stupid creature he was. He felt superior to be called Master, and never doubted Muna was telling the truth. He waddled across the hall behind her and down the cellar steps, treading on her mattress and crushing it. Without a bulb in the cellar light, he couldn't see as well as Muna, but there was enough brightness from the hall to show him how she reached through the metal rack and pushed the door to the second chamber open. He gave a gasp of astonishment.

Muna sank to her knees on the floor. Please be kind, Master, she begged, holding out her hands. Princess lets me eat so little that I'll die if you steal everything that's in there.

Abiola moved forward, eyes full of curiosity. You'd better hope I don't tell Mamma this cupboard exists. You're not allowed to have secrets.

Muna believed the Devil reached out to pull him inside and slam the door closed, but once or twice she had flashbacks of memory where she leaped on his back and dug her fingers into his eyes to send him staggering into the darkness. She had no doubt about the deep, raucous laughter that filled her ears afterwards.

Once she'd washed the soiled sheets, cleaned the kitchen and made a new creamy chocolate pudding for Yetunde, she picked up the rod and collected Abiola's lunch box and schoolbag from where he'd left them on the sideboard in the hall. She didn't need a torch. She could see in the dark, and would beat him if he tried to attack her. But he was dead. And Muna was glad.

He lay now as he'd lain then, fully clothed and curled in a ball with his eyes shut and his thumb in his mouth. Beside him were the lunch box and the schoolbag. Muna thought she could love him quite easily like this. Yetunde, too, who looked kind and motherly leaning against her suitcase, her right hand reaching out to the son she'd lost.

There was no smell, not even from the urine that had soaked Yetunde's skirt. Muna wondered if the Devil had built this cool, airless chamber for that purpose – to keep the bodies of her enemies whole and clean for her to enjoy. She shone the torch into Yetunde's handbag to find the wallet and remove the credit card. Then, as carefully as she'd done each time before, she closed the door and tiptoed backwards, using a soft brush to swirl dust over the footprints that showed she'd walked through a wall.

She squatted in the corner of her room that night, staring at Yetunde's smartphone and the two small squares of plastic on the carpet in front of her. She had taken the mobile and Ebuka's credit card after he fell asleep, but she was still undecided whether to use his number or Yetunde's to buy food. The gulf in her understanding of how such small, lifeless things could speak was huge.

The decision would have been removed from her if Ebuka hadn't stirred when she returned from Mrs Hughes. He'd opened his eyes as she stood looking down at him, and she'd had to pretend the mobile had slipped from his lap as he dozed. She stooped as if to pick it up and her chance of ordering the food then, using the card he kept in his wallet beside his bed, was lost.

Now she didn't know which to choose. Ebuka had said he would know Yetunde was alive if she spent money. But was that enough? What else might the card tell Ebuka? She lifted it and held it close to her face, wondering how it could even say it belonged to Yetunde. Where was its voice?

Muna's lack of expression and long schooling in patience served her well the next day. With no idea when the white van would come, or even if she had succeeded in placing an order, she stretched the food Mrs Hughes had given her and listened calmly to Ebuka's frustrations.

He felt belittled because the credit-card company had refused to give him the information he wanted. At Yetunde's insistence, he had made her the primary cardholder so she could deal direct with the company if questions of fraud arose. It had seemed wise at the time. Yetunde knew Ebuka's shopping habits – he was predictable – and she would recognise a criminal transaction immediately. The same could not be said of him.

Muna was kneading dough for flatbreads from the flour Mrs Hughes had given her. What does all that mean, Master?

Yetunde never gave me the security password. Only she can be told how the card's being used. I pay the bill but I have no rights.

Does that make you angry, Master?

Ebuka gave a sour smile. It'll teach me to keep control next time. They told me one thing at least, but only because I said I was worried my wife had had an accident. The last transaction was at two o'clock this morning.

Is that good, Master?

It says she's hasn't lost her taste for spending money . . . though God knows what she was buying in the early hours. She never stays awake beyond ten.

She watches the shopping channels, Master. I've seen her buy many things from the television when she's unhappy.

More likely she's with her sister, and the pair of them are draining the account. There's no containing Yetunde when she's in this sort of mood. She won't stop until the card reaches its limit . . . which it will when I refuse to pay it off.

Muna nodded as if she understood. Yes, Master.

Ebuka muttered that all he'd ever been good for was paying bills, and it was time Yetunde learned those days were over. After that he had other things to preoccupy him. The nurse came. She was glad to hear he and his daughter had made an excursion to the High Street but she tut-tutted at the shortage of disposable gloves and swabs. Mr Songoli should have used the opportunity to buy supplies. She gave Muna some replacements but told Ebuka that hygiene and cleanliness were his responsibility. It was no excuse to say his wife was away for a few days. There were plenty of pharmacies close by, and it would be good therapy to go out and make the purchases himself.

Ebuka pretended to agree. Muna would take him later, he said. But the nurse shook her head, telling the girl she must encourage her father to make the trip alone. Coping with disability was as much about building confidence as managing bedsores and catheters. She watched Ebuka demonstrate how easily he could now move from his bed to his chair, and urged him to build on this new independence. He couldn't rely on his wife and daughter all his life.

Later, Muna took Ebuka's jacket and gloves to the sitting room and urged him to do as the nurse had suggested. She couched her request in the terms the woman had used – the Master would build his confidence by going out alone – but her motives were selfish. Ebuka's absence from the house would spare her having to invent explanations when the white van came. If necessary, she would find more reasons to send him out tomorrow.

Ebuka took food for granted – it was always there – but he would be curious if a man arrived with plastic bags. Who had told him to come, he would ask, and Muna feared the man would answer that the order came from Yetunde's phone and was paid for by her card. For every problem she solved, another arose.

She was too persistent in her attempts to persuade Ebuka from the house. He accused her of nagging and said he would make the decision in his own good time. With a small shrug, she left the room, closing the door behind her, but her heart hardened against him. She had done everything she could to spare Ebuka harm, and the fault would be his if the Devil punished him for making little Muna's troubles more onerous.

Fifteen

Olubayo came home from school and leered at her from the kitchen doorway as she pulled the last of the flesh from the chicken carcase to make soup. He rubbed his groin against the doorjamb, and Muna bared her teeth at him, hissing loudly. He took no notice. She'd lost her power to scare him since his father had started listening to what he had to say. If he'd ever believed that Ebuka had killed Abiola, or that demons lived in the walls of the cellar, he didn't any more.

Where's Dada? he demanded.

Muna watched him out of the corner of her eye. The Master went to the shops as the nurse instructed him to do, she said.

When's he coming back?

When he has what he needs.

Olubayo's eyes filled with lust. It was the first time he and Muna had been alone in the house since Abiola went missing. He moved into the room, unzipping his fly. I know you want me. Ask what I can give you. Tell me you're a slut and a whore.

Muna had heard such phrases coming out of his computer. They made no sense to her. She picked up the heavy saucepan and cradled it against her chest. I have no use for you at all. I'd like it better if you weren't here.

He pulled out his penis. You'll wish you hadn't said that when I make you swallow this.

Muna looked at the engorged and filthy thing with its glistening head. Was this what Ebuka had put in her mouth? Bile rose in her throat as she lowered the saucepan to her side to swing it. She was too slow. Olubayo was upon her, knocking the weapon from her grasp and slamming the weight of his other fist against the side of her head.

Muna slumped to the ground, curling herself into a tight ball. He tugged at her clothes, her arms, her hair in an attempt to turn her into one of the amenable rag dolls he saw on his computer screen, but Muna knew from Yetunde's attacks that the damage would be less if she kept herself small. He growled as he kicked her, voicing his frustration in animal-like grunts, calling her a fucking bitch and a cock-teaser.

It seemed an age before Ebuka rescued her. He swung the rod against his son's back and then drove it into Olubayo's midriff as the boy turned with a howl of shock. But Ebuka was mistaken if he thought his son would recognise his authority. Hot with rage, Olubayo grasped the rod and threatened to pull his father from his chair if he didn't let go.

I'm no different from you, he snarled. Do you think me and Abiola didn't know she sucked you off whenever you felt like it? Do you think Mamma didn't know? She thought it was funny. She slept better after she gave you the piccaninny to fuck.

He knew a brief triumph as his father shrank away from him but his gloating expression turned to pained surprise as something sharp was thrust into the muscle of his right arm. He stared at his father in confusion, unsure what was happening, then let go of the rod as the blade was wrenched free. He pulled away, gasps of shock issuing from his mouth, and Muna's second strike glanced off his ribs instead of plunging into his side.

She dropped the small Japanese paring knife into the sink and pulled a larger one from the wooden block on the worktop. She inspected it for a moment, as if wondering why she was holding it; then, without warning, she dropped into a cat-like crouch and jumped at Olubayo, her lips drawn back in a snarl. With a shout of alarm Ebuka pushed his son aside and raised the rod. Enough! he cried. Don't make me hit you, Muna! Olubayo is sorry for hurting you.

Muna straightened. From the bowels of the earth she heard the faint echo of the Devil's laugh. Olubayo is never sorry for what he does, Master. I ache all over from where he kicked me. Only you have ever said you were wrong to treat little Muna with cruelty.

Ebuka glanced at the boy. Apologise, he ordered. You behaved badly.

But Olubayo refused. Why do you take her side? he demanded angrily. She's made me bleed. He took his hand from where it was clutching the wound on his arm and showed the blood on his palm. If you cared about me, you'd order her to the cellar and call the police.

Ebuka's tone was scornful. Has epilepsy turned you into an imbecile? How will you explain why she attacked you? Look at yourself. You're undone and there's semen on your trousers. Do you want it known that you tried to rape your sister?

A dark flush burned the boy's cheeks as he pulled up his zip. She's not my sister. She's *no one* . . . just a fucking *slave*.

Then call the police yourself. She'll receive more kindness from them than you or I will. We'll go to prison while she goes to a welcoming home. Are you too stupid to understand that?

Olubayo stamped his foot. It wasn't me who stole her. I *hate* her. I've always hated her. *Abiola* hated her. You give her more love than you ever gave us.

With a sigh of despair, Ebuka lowered the rod. You have your mother's jealousy. She destroyed us all by what she did. I should have sent Muna back to the orphanage when Yetunde first brought her home – it's what I wanted to do – but I allowed myself to be persuaded it was a good thing to offer shelter to an abandoned child.

You kept her because you liked fucking her, the boy cried, clutching his arm again. She liked it too or she'd have told the police on you.

Ebuka shook his head, remembering Muna's pitiless face when he begged for her help in the cellar. Be grateful she didn't, he snapped. Your parents would have been lost to you if she'd told the truth. Is that your wish? To become as unloved and unwanted as she was? You'll achieve it easily enough by whining that a slave hurt you when you tried to rape her.

Olubayo's face contorted with conflicting emotions. He wanted Muna punished but he didn't want to be punished himself, and Muna saw in his eyes that he would never forget the pain she'd caused him. She saw too that he hadn't understood his father's words as well as she had. She addressed Ebuka.

This silly boy frightens me, Master. He's not clever and he still believes his size and strength make him more powerful than me. Yet I have only to tell the witchy-white that Princess made me her prisoner and every Songoli will be condemned.

Did you understand that when the police first came to the house?

No, Master. I was afraid they meant me harm. Princess taught me to fear strangers, particularly whites.

Would you have told them the truth if you hadn't feared them?

I don't believe so, Master. My life has been better since you claimed me as your daughter.

I'm glad, Muna. If I can make amends for the harm my family has done you, I will.

She fixed him with her solemn gaze. I don't want Olubayo for a brother, Master. It would make me happier if he wasn't here.

Olubayo moved forward, clenching his fists in fury, but Ebuka raised the rod to hold him back. She says nothing you haven't said, he growled. Do you imagine her hatred for you is any less than yours for her . . . and with more reason? You behaved like an animal.

Olubayo wasn't so dull-witted he couldn't recognise hypocrisy when he heard it. His eyes filled with angry tears. I did only what you've done a thousand times, he cried. Can't you see she wants rid of me so that she can have you for herself? You're the only one she likes.

A small gleam of pleasure entered Ebuka's eyes as he looked towards Muna, and, with a howl of pain, Olubayo fled from the room.

Muna turned back to the chicken carcase. You should go after him and clean his wound, Master. He will call an ambulance and cause trouble for you otherwise. I shall pray for his temper and unhappiness to bring on a seizure so that he forgets what

127

happened here. There'll be no need to call a doctor. I know what to do because Princess showed me.

The Devil's laughter made the floorboards shake beneath Muna's bed that night. She thrilled as the deep bass rumble travelled through the house and into her mattress. Everything she'd hoped for had come to pass. Olubayo had tried to use the phone, and Ebuka had struck him on the side of his head before he could use it. The boy had fallen to the ground, twitching and frothing, and Muna had knelt beside him, loosening his clothes and turning him on to his side when the seizure calmed.

She spoke kindly to him as she eased his arm from his school uniform to clean and bandage his wound, and when his wits returned she told him he had hurt himself as he fell. Of course he believed her. He had no memory of anything else. At Muna's urging, Ebuka expressed concern for his son, and Olubayo, dazed and disorientated, said he was sorry for being a nuisance and wept with gratitude for their sympathy and understanding.

Muna congratulated herself on the smiles Ebuka gave him for she knew them to be false. He would never feel sympathy for this weak-minded son. Everything Olubayo did reminded him of his own behaviour. Worse, he felt shamed by the boy's epilepsy, knowing Songoli blood was the cause. The beatings Muna had taken were far worse yet her thoughts remained strong and clear.

You have a generous nature, Ebuka told her after Olubayo had gone to bed. You were more caring than he deserved.

He can't help himself, Master. He must act as you and Princess have taught him. Just as Abiola did.

Why are you different? The lessons you received were far more brutal.

I've learned that hate and cruelty achieve nothing, Master.

The van came early the next morning when only Muna was awake. The driver brought the plastic bags into the hall and told her to ask Mrs Songoli to sign the receipt. Muna said Mamma was ill, and begged the man to make the signature for her. Mamma would be unhappy if he took the food away again. Having incurred Yetunde's displeasure on several occasions in the past when items she'd ordered had been omitted or were of poor quality, he did.

Once the cupboards and fridge were full, Muna made breakfast for Ebuka and took it to him on a tray. She informed him Olubayo was still asleep and said she didn't want to wake him. The boy's mood was never good in the morning. It would be better if he was allowed to stay home for a day so that she could mend the cut in the blazer sleeve and clean the blood from it.

Ebuka rubbed the sleep from his bleary eyes and told her to do whatever she liked. He was out of patience with his son.

Sixteen

While Muna helped Ebuka dress, he declared his intention of going to a pharmacy to purchase supplies. She shook her head.

You can't, Master. You must wait until tomorrow when Olubayo is back at school. He'll attack me again if he finds me alone.

You shouldn't have lied to him yesterday. You knew I was in the house.

I wanted you to find out what he's like, Master. I knew he'd behave as he did if he thought you'd gone to the shops.

Has he done it before?

Only once, Master. He was too afraid of Princess to try again. She knocked him down when she caught him in the kitchen with his trousers undone. She said it was my fault for encouraging him . . . and beat me also.

Ebuka studied her for a moment. Was Princess right? Did you do something to make Olubayo think you liked him in that way?

In what way, Master?

Did you give him the impression you thought it would be nice to be kissed or touched by him?

Muna stared back, unblinking. You know I did not, Master. It frightens me to be touched. A sickness rises in my belly when it happens for I know I will suffer pain. Isn't that the lesson you and Princess wanted me to learn?

She saw guilt and discomfort in Ebuka's eyes before he turned his chair and wheeled himself to the sitting room, muttering that he'd speak to Olubayo later. But, as the hours passed, he showed no inclination to call his son downstairs. He didn't want any more accusations that he'd committed the same offences himself, and Muna despised him for his weakness. Ebuka would do as Yetunde had done if the subject were raised again. Blame little Muna. Had he not done so already?

When lunchtime came, she asked him what she should do with Olubayo's food and he told her to keep it warm in the kitchen. There was no point rushing the boy. The seizure must have made him sleepy. He would come down when he was ready.

Muna didn't argue. It suited her well if he preferred to let Olubayo remain in his room. Just once, she reminded Ebuka that he should phone the school to say his son was unwell but Ebuka resisted, fearing a bossy woman on the other end. He excused himself by saying it was a poor place. If they'd noticed Olubayo was missing, they'd have called him. He would send a note with the boy tomorrow.

The light outside was beginning to fade before Ebuka came to the kitchen and asked Muna to go upstairs to find out what Olubayo was doing. She was sponging the sleeve of the blazer to remove the blood, and shook her head as she pressed a clean towel to the fabric to dry it.

He's doing what he always does, Master: watching dirty things on his computer. If I enter his room, he will do them to me.

I'm not asking you to enter. Call to him and say his father wants to speak to him.

You can do that yourself, Master. He'll take more notice of you than of me.

He's two floors up. He won't hear me if his speakers are playing.

Then you must shout loudly, Master.

Ebuka glared at her, unused to refusals. You go too far, he snapped. You're behaving like this because Princess isn't here. You wouldn't expect *her* to choose you over her son, would you?

I don't ask you to choose, Master. I warn you, that is all. If Olubayo comes near me again I will use a bigger knife against him. It matters little to me if he dies. The police won't blame a frightened slave for protecting herself, not when they know the painful things you did to me in the cellar and how you taught your son to do the same.

That's not true.

All boys learn from their fathers, Master.

Ebuka's expression swung between anger and uncertainty. They won't believe you. They'll want to know why you didn't tell them this before and why you pretended to be my daughter. You've told as many lies as I have.

I've told none, Master. I was never asked if I was your daughter.

You lied about being able to understand English.

Princess did that, Master. She said I was too stupid to learn and everyone believed her, yourself included. When she returns she'll be shocked to find how much cleverer I am than her worthless sons.

You'd better learn to curb your tongue before she does. She'll beat the arrogance out of you if you try to speak to her like this.

Yes, Master.

Ebuka wheeled himself into the hall and began shouting for Olubayo. When the boy didn't answer or appear, Ebuka rained threats and curses on his head for daring to defy his father's authority. Muna listened impassively for a moment or two and then closed the kitchen door. From one of the cupboards she took a bag of sugared almonds and popped the sweeties one at a time into her mouth.

It had always been her ambition to grow fat and lazy like Yetunde.

Muna held out her hands in a begging gesture when Mrs Hughes opened her front door. 'I need you to come to our house, lady,' she whispered. 'Dada needs your help.'

A man appeared from the sitting room. 'Who is it, darling?'

'The girl I told you about.' Mrs Hughes caught Muna's hand to prevent her retreating. 'Don't be afraid,' she said. 'My husband won't harm you.'

Muna allowed herself to be drawn on to the doorstep. She had known Mr Hughes would be there because she had seen his car on the driveway. For six years she had watched him drive to and fro. He had snow-white hair and wore grey suits. His favourite shirts were pale pink and his favourite ties dark blue.

She ducked her head. 'It pleases me to meet you, sir. I see you sometimes from Dada's windows.'

Mr Hughes joined his wife, his eyes creasing in a concerned smile at the frail child who hovered like a wraith in the reflected orange light from the street. 'Come in,' he invited. 'Tell us what we can do for you.'

But Muna remained silent and Mrs Hughes answered for her. 'She said her father needs help. Why, child? Is he ill?'

'I'm not sure, lady. He's lying outside Olubayo's door. He didn't believe me when I said Olubayo wasn't in his room . . . and pulled himself to the top floor to make sure. He's worn himself out and I don't know what to do.'

'Has your mother come home?'

Muna shook her head. 'Dada thinks she must have spoken to Olubayo at his school yesterday. My brother was very angry when he came home last night – called Dada terrible names – and now he isn't in the house any more.'

Mrs Hughes made what she could of these statements. 'Your father thinks Olubayo's gone to be with his mother?'

'Yes, lady. He's taken his rucksack and some things belonging to Dada that Mamma always wanted for herself. '

'What things?'

'The gold circlets and bracelets that Dada's father gave him, lady. Mamma said if Dada didn't wear them, he should give them to her . . . but he said they were too valuable and didn't want them lost or stolen.'

Mr Hughes lifted a couple of coats from a chair in the hall, handing one to his wife and shrugging his arms into the other. 'We should go,' he told her. 'There'll be time for explanations later.'

At first Muna found Mr Hughes less frightening than his wife. His eyes didn't search hers the way Mrs Hughes's did, and his only interest seemed to be in how he could help Ebuka. But as she took them inside and led them upstairs, she noticed how boldly he looked into every room and how easily he assumed control. Ebuka lay on his side in front of Olubayo's open door and Muna knelt beside him, stroking his brow and telling him she'd brought help.

Ebuka gripped Mr Hughes's hand, relieved to see a man he recognised. He repeated what Muna had said, that he'd used his arms to hoist himself up a step at a time and was now exhausted. He'd been foolish to embark on such an endeavour. It was one thing to pull his unresponsive legs up behind him, quite another to manoeuvre them down again. He begged Mr Hughes to assist him rather than call an ambulance. There was nothing wrong with him, bar a little fatigue, and he couldn't bear to parade his stupidity before paramedics.

It seemed to Muna that Mrs Hughes was about to protest, but her husband nodded and hooked his right arm through Ebuka's to pull him into a sitting position. 'My father-in-law had the same problem each time his chair lift broke,' he said reassuringly. 'We discovered the best method was to work our way down in tandem. I'll sit in front of you to manage your legs but you'll have to take your weight on your elbows to lower yourself. If you get tired we'll pause.'

He sent Muna ahead of them, and she watched as they eased, tread by tread, down each flight of stairs. Mr Hughes sat two steps below, supporting Ebuka's dead legs on his shoulders and giving the instruction to move. By taking half the weight, there was less stress on his passenger's arms, and Ebuka, delighting in the progress they made, paid no heed to what Mrs Hughes was doing.

Not so Muna. She listened to the telltale creak of floorboards as the witchy-white tiptoed from room to room, and she thought Mr Hughes cunning and clever to give his wife time to poke her inquisitive nose into places it shouldn't go. There was nothing to find. Muna had even remembered to place Olubayo's epilepsy pills beside his toothbrush and flannel in his rucksack.

The wooden box which had contained Ebuka's jewellery stood open on Olubayo's desk, with a few valueless items still in it, and empty coat hangers hung in the open wardrobe with the clothes Olubayo hadn't wanted – mostly his uniform – dropped carelessly on the floor. The lights were on, the curtains closed and the bed unruffled as if it hadn't been used. To the most suspicious eye, the room looked as if its owner had waited until the rest of the house was asleep before taking what he needed and creeping downstairs to remove his passport from the sideboard on his way out.

Ebuka was tearfully grateful for his neighbour's help once he was safely back in his chair in the hall, expressing embarrassment for calling him out on a cold evening. Mr Hughes told him to think nothing of it – *what else were friends for?* – and Ebuka's eyes welled again. Muna made her own thanks more quietly, smiling shyly at Mr Hughes and then at his witchy wife as she came down the stairs. There was nothing to alarm her in either face but she guessed Mr Hughes had only kept the ambulance away to persuade Ebuka to answer his questions. They were very direct.

When had Olubayo left? Why had Mr Songoli waited so long to check his room? Was what Muna said true, that the boy had come home angry from school and called his father names? If so, why? And what had been said that might cause him to leave?

Ebuka shook his head and wept, expressing ignorance about everything except whether Muna was telling the truth. 'I've never seen the boy in such a temper. He tried to do what my wife did . . . pull me from the chair. It made me think he must have spoken to her. You've seen for yourself I'm quite helpless when I'm on the floor.'

'But if he called you names you must have some idea what he was accusing you of. '

'He was jealous. He said I've always favoured Muna over him. I dread to think what damage he'd have done to us if he hadn't had a seizure.' He glanced towards the sitting room. 'Muna said he'd have no memory of what he'd done when he came to, and she was right. He'd forgotten everything. As far as I know, he went to bed happy.'

Mr Hughes glanced at the girl. 'Is your father right? Did Olubayo seem happy to you?'

Muna wriggled her shoulders. 'He was happy that Dada was kind to him, sir, but not happy that he fell to the ground. His epilepsy shames him.'

'Weren't you worried when he didn't come down this morning?'

'Not really, sir. Mamma never makes him go to school after a seizure. We thought he was sleeping.'

'Why didn't you check?'

Muna gave a small shrug. 'I didn't want to. He said bad things to me too last night.'

The man looked amused. 'So you were as cross with your brother as he was with you? Are you a little jealous as well? Do you think your mother favours him over you?'

'Yes, sir. She likes men better than ladies.'

'She must have been very upset when Abiola went missing.'

'She cried for him every day, and then Dada had his accident and she said we should never have come here. She wanted to go home to Africa but we couldn't . . . not while Dada was in hospital.'

'Who looked after your father when he was released?'

Muna lowered her head in pretended discomfort. 'Mamma did, sir.'

There was a short silence before Ebuka spoke. 'She's lying,' he said bluntly. 'My wife found everything to do with my disability abhorrent. Muna's been caring for me from the day I got back.' Abruptly, he wheeled his chair to the sideboard and pulled open the drawer, searching in vain for Olubayo's passport. 'She was always planning to leave and take my son with her. I see that now.' The ever-ready tears sprang into his eyes again. 'She's been blaming me for everything since Abiola was taken.'

Mr Hughes made a gesture of sympathy. 'Your whole family should have been given grief counselling. Was it ever offered?'

Ebuka shook his head. 'It would have made no difference. Yetunde wouldn't have accepted it. She doesn't like strangers knowing our business.'

Muna turned to the witchy-white. 'What is grief counselling, lady?'

'Help with coming to terms with the loss of a loved one. Your mother would have learned to cope with her sorrow for Abiola.'

'She felt more sorry for herself, lady. It shamed her to be married to a cripple.'

'That's not a good word, Muna.'

'Is it not, lady? I learned it from Mamma when she told Mr Broadstone she would leave Dada as soon as the money came from the police and the ambulance men. Is "spaz" better? That's what the boys at Olubayo's school called Dada. It made Olubayo cry . . .

even more when they said he was a "fucktard" for being epileptic. Would grief counselling have helped with these sorrows?'

Mrs Hughes looked to her husband to answer, but once again it was Ebuka who broke the silence. 'Mr Broadstone's our solicitor,' he explained. 'He persuaded Yetunde we'd be successful if we brought negligence claims – she's been pinning her hopes on it – but he wrote just before she left to say the case looks flawed now that he's seen the official records. I should have guessed that's what caused her anger. She thought she could lie her way to a fortune.'

Mr Hughes made another – smaller – gesture of sympathy. 'I'm sorry,' he said. 'It looks as if you have some hard decisions to make . . . the first being whether to report your son missing. If he's with his mother, the police won't be interested, I'm afraid. They don't get involved in custody disputes.'

Seventeen

Ebuka swung between certainty and doubt as the days passed. In public, he was certain Olubayo was with Yetunde. In private, he expressed his doubts to Muna. He informed Olubayo's school that his son had returned to Africa with his mother but told Muna that Princess's sister had denied it when he called her on the telephone. She hadn't seen Yetunde in six years and blamed Ebuka for being too mean to pay for holidays.

Muna massaged his calf. I expect she's lying, Master. If you knew where Princess was, you'd insist on talking to Olubayo. Princess wouldn't want that.

Why not?

You'd tell him you loved him and he'd beg his mother to let him come back.

I miss him, Muna.

I know, Master. Princess knows it, too. That's why she doesn't want you to find him. She likes hurting you.

On the third day, a female Education Officer knocked on the door, requesting explanations. There were rules governing education. It was a fineable offence to remove a child during term time except for the most extreme and urgent of circumstances.

Mr Songoli must produce documents: a letter setting out the emergency, a booking confirmation from an airline, an address and phone number for the mother and the boy. It would become a criminal matter if Mr Songoli had sent Olubayo abroad for the purposes of forced marriage.

Ebuka flushed purple with anger. Was this a racist slur because he was black? Did officials in this terrible country think his ambitions for his thirteen-year-old son were so low that he'd force him to take on the responsibility of a wife? And what right did this woman have to enter his house and lecture him when he wasn't a British citizen? It was none of her business if his son chose to live with his mother in the country where he was born. This created more problems for him. It seemed foreign nationals from non-EU countries weren't entitled to state-funded education. Had Mr Songoli applied to the Home Office for permission to bypass this rule? If so, where was the letter granting his son a free education at the taxpayers' expense? The woman turned her attention to Muna. And why was his daughter not in school? In a free, equal and open society, girls were expected to be educated to the same standard as boys.

It fell to Muna to beg the woman for understanding. She took her by the hand and led her into the hall, pleading with her in whispers not to be angry with Dada. He'd been ill in hospital when Mamma had put Olubayo in his new school, and Mamma knew nothing about rules. She was a good woman and had done what she thought was right. It was her brother's last school – the expensive one – that had lost Abiola, and Mamma was afraid the same thing would happen to Olubayo. They had all suffered so badly after Abiola was stolen. It was hard to be sensible when grief was overwhelming.

The woman softened. 'Do you know where your mother and brother are, Muna?'

'Yes, lady. They're with Mamma's family. She became too afraid of white people to stay here.'

'Why didn't you and your father go with them?'

'Dada's not strong enough to travel long distances, lady. The nurse says he might be one day . . . but not now.' She gave a small apologetic shrug. 'Mamma was pleased to leave him behind. She said cruel things to him about not being a man any more . . . and told him it would shame her if her family saw him as he is.'

The woman looked uncomfortable. 'Was Olubayo happy about leaving?'

'I believe so, lady. He's always loved Mamma better because she gives him what he wants. He called Dada terrible names, saying he's of no use to us any more . . . and Dada cried.'

'Did your mother blame your father for Abiola's loss?'

'No, lady. Only white people like you. She thought it was safe for Abiola to go to school in your country, but it wasn't.'

The woman looked past her towards the front door. 'I expect she blames herself. Mothers never get over their children being taken.'

'Perhaps, lady.'

'Are you upset that she left you behind?'

Muna shook her head. 'She said I'd have to marry a stranger if I went with her. There wouldn't be enough money otherwise. I'd rather be with Dada. I love him very much.'

'But it's not a suitable arrangement. You should be in school.'

'Is that what your rules say, lady? If so, I find them strange. How will Dada pay when you've told him his children can't be taught for free? It's hard to do things correctly here when' – she searched her memory for the right term – '*taxpayers* get as angry as Mamma because a man becomes a cripple.' She saw pain in the woman's eyes. 'I'm sorry, lady. Should I have said "spaz"? I've yet to learn which word whites prefer for a man who isn't a man any more.'

A sickly smile distorted the woman's face. 'Disabled.'

Muna repeated it. 'Dis-abled. Is that the same as *un*-able, lady? Dada is unable to please his wife so she's gone to find a better husband somewhere else? Is that what it means?'

'You shouldn't speak of your father's problems so openly, Muna. It's not polite.'

'But it's why Mamma left him, lady. She said she needs a man who can love her properly.'

With a cowardly glance towards the sitting room, the woman reached for the front-door handle. 'Tell Mr Songoli I won't be recommending any further action in regard to your brother . . . but I urge you to persuade him to consult a lawyer about his rights, particularly in relation to his disability. It's quite wrong if he feels marginalised and disrespected because of it.'

Muna thanked her and watched with satisfaction as she scurried down the driveway to her car. It was good that whites found the truth embarrassing. It made them easier to get rid of.

Ebuka began to notice that Muna spent less time with him. He criticised her for it, demanding to know what she did when she went upstairs. She said she was cleaning the house as she always did, and made no mention of dressing in Yetunde's clothes, smoothing Yetunde's creams into her face and lying on Yetunde's bed to watch Yetunde's little television and eat bonbons.

The rooms upstairs and everything in them belonged to her now, and it pleased her to move from one to the other, exulting in her new possessions. Ebuka's demands bored her. He must learn to do things for himself.

She thought him very slow-witted each time he tried to impose his will on her. He should know by now that her determination was stronger than his. She could squat for ever in a corner, watching him spit fury at her, but he lacked the patience even to keep his mouth shut for half an hour.

He looked to the nurse to intervene on his behalf, criticising Muna churlishly for denying him help when he needed it. He told the woman his daughter found it amusing to leave everything he needed out of reach, principally his chair. Muna explained timidly that she was trying to encourage his confidence, and the nurse took her side, scolding Ebuka for expecting Muna to act as an unpaid servant.

Muna loved to see the despair in Ebuka's eyes at times like these. He could have said that Muna had the key to his door and came and went as she pleased. That she removed the chair each night, locked him in for hour after hour when it suited her and tortured him by leaving him to starve. That even if he could escape his bed and room, he had no means of phoning for help because Muna kept the computers, the mobiles and the handset for the landline upstairs.

But he said none of these things for he knew Muna's punishments were easier to bear than the whites' revulsion if Muna ever revealed he'd emptied his filth into a frail little slave because his fat, ugly wife didn't like him emptying it into her.

Eighteen

Muna stooped over Ebuka's bed to peer into his face when the bill from the credit-card company arrived. He seemed shocked.

What's wrong, Master? Has Princess spent more than you thought she would?

He made a grab for her throat but Muna was too quick for him. She jumped away, wondering what he expected to achieve by such an action. Did he think he could force her into obedience by hurting her? Or that he'd be better off if he killed her? The phones and computers would still be out of his reach. She watched as he took long, calming breaths.

I don't believe Yetunde's used the card at all, he said. There are two transactions at the local supermarket but no hotels or airline tickets.

I expect that's why she asked Olubayo to steal your jewellery, Master. She wanted to sell it so that she could buy things without you knowing.

A flicker of impatience crossed Ebuka's face. I told you when Princess left that I'd know something had happened to her if she didn't use her card.

But she has, Master. She's bought food for herself and Olubayo.

Someone has . . . but I don't think it's Princess. My guess is her card's been stolen. Why would she be shopping in our local supermarket if she's in Africa?

Perhaps she didn't go to Africa, Master.

He tapped the page angrily. Then where are the payments for rent or hotels? She can't stay in England without having some-where to live. There should be a hundred transactions recorded here.

She's staying with a friend, Master. She must be close if she was able to talk to Olubayo.

Ebuka searched her face, his eyes deeply troubled. If I thought it possible, I'd believe you were responsible for Yetunde and Olubayo leaving . . . even Abiola's disappearance. You've gained more each time than anyone else.

Muna stared back at him. I've gained nothing, Master. I'm still a slave.

You don't behave like one.

But what could I have done to make Princess and Olubayo leave, Master? They never did anything they didn't want to do. I can't make people vanish just by wishing.

He clenched and unclenched his fists. But you'd like to. You'd live here alone if you could. You're more attached to this house than you've ever been to a person. I see the look of triumph on your face when you stand in the hall and think of it as yours.

It cares for me as much as I have cared for it, Master.

Houses don't have feelings, Muna.

This one does, Master. I hear its laughter sometimes.

He looked away from her towards the window, and Muna saw how fiercely he was debating with himself. She guessed he knew it was she who had used Yetunde's card, for even a man as stupid as Ebuka must question eventually where his food came from. But, no. When he spoke it was about the house.

Do you hope to stay here for ever, Muna?

It's my home, Master. I like it here.

But do you understand that it doesn't belong to me? It's owned by someone else, who expects me to pay him rent.

What is rent, Master?

Money.

We have that, Master.

Not for much longer. My salary is only guaranteed for another month. When it stops coming we'll be unable to stay. This house is too big and the rent's too high. We shall have to move somewhere cheaper.

Muna pictured the bodies in the cellar. I don't want that, Master.

We'll be evicted if we try to stay. Landlords have no interest in tenants who can't pay what they owe. We'll be forced to leave whether we like it or not.

You must find a way to keep paying, Master.

Ebuka turned back to her with a hollow laugh. How? Where do you think money comes from? If Princess were here, she'd be on her phone to my employer, begging him to let me work from home on my computer . . . or asking the council to pay our rent. She wouldn't lose the house through ignorance as you are doing.

A tiny flicker of uncertainty sparked in Muna's mind. Was he telling the truth or trying to lure her into giving him a telephone? She recalled Mr Broadstone saying once that it was a pity Ebuka hadn't taken out a mortgage and insured himself against accident. Once paralysed, the debt would have been paid off, and his wife would have had one less thing to worry about. The words had meant nothing to Muna because she didn't understand them, but she saw they gave Yetunde yet another reason to demand compensation.

She watched Ebuka closely. Princess would be calling Mr Broadstone, Master. He said every time he came that he could win money for her. You should talk to him before you talk to your employer.

She was so certain Ebuka was trying to trick her into giving him his mobile that she didn't think he'd remember what he'd told Mr Hughes. She was wrong. He shook his head irritably.

The lawyer's already said the case won't stand up. You're as naïve as Yetunde if you think there's an easy way to stay here. We must find someone else to help us.

Not we, Master . . . *you*.

But I can do nothing while you keep me prisoner and deny me access to my phone and my laptop. I assume it's your way of punishing me but it's hardly clever. You can't stay here without me.

Muna knew this to be true. She dreamed often of pitching Ebuka down the cellar steps but she recognised that his death would cause more problems than it solved. However much she wanted the house to herself, she could think of no good explanation for why her crippled father would leave without her or how he could make a journey on his own. All manner of busybodies would come asking questions – the witchy-white more than anyone.

Also she doubted her ability to drag Ebuka's heavy, lifeless body into the second chamber when it had been so hard to move

Olubayo's. The boy, still grateful for her kindness after his seizure, had followed her downstairs in the middle of the night when she told him Yetunde had left a message on the landline that his father didn't want him to hear.

Olubayo was very stupid. Muna persuaded him to descend in silence and darkness so that Ebuka wouldn't wake, and, yawning constantly, he didn't see the open cellar door or the hammer that smashed against the side of his head. He fell and tumbled to the Devil's laughter just as his mother had, and Muna thrilled to see him crumpled on the stone floor when she switched on the light.

She crept down the steps, eager to remind him that she'd said she hadn't wanted him for a brother. But he was dead, and the job of dragging and rolling his limp body to the hidden door was arduous and tiring, leaving blood trails on the stones which had to be cleaned and carefully covered with dust when they were dry. Of course little Muna did it well. She did everything well, but she would have to be bigger and stronger before she could do the same with Ebuka.

Did you ever try to punish Yetunde? Ebuka asked suddenly.

I would if I'd been able, Master, but she was too big for someone as small as me. You'd have found me dead on the floor if I'd tried. She came close to killing me many times.

Ebuka gave a weary sigh, knowing she was right. She made monsters of us all the day she went to the orphanage, he said. She found your name in an old newspaper, which is why she was able to forge documents, claiming a relationship with you.

Why was I in the newspaper, Master?

Your mother was murdered when you were four years old. The nuns took you in and gave you a home.

Why don't I remember my mother, Master?

149

Your experience was traumatic. You cradled her head in your lap for three days before neighbours came to check on you. The smell of death alerted them that something was wrong.

I have no recollection of it, Master.

Shock robbed you of speech and memory. The nuns described you as the most silent child they'd ever had, and advised Princess you would never be able to communicate fully. It was they who suggested you might have suffered brain damage at birth.

Did they find the murderer, Master?

Ebuka shook his head. Your mother knew many men. The police were never able to discover which of them killed her.

Did they try, Master?

Not as hard as they should. She brought shame on herself by the way she earned her money.

Muna pictured the naked women on Olubayo's computer. Princess said my mother was her sister, Master.

Only because it suited her purpose. She spun a story about a second wife who allowed her daughter to go to the bad and lose contact with the rest of the family. She told the nuns she'd only recently learned that your mother was dead. If she'd known earlier, she'd have rescued you sooner. She lied well and they believed her.

Who is my father, Master?

I don't know. The neighbours said your mother didn't either.

Muna's unblinking eyes stared at him. Why are you telling me this, Master?

Because it's better you know your story before the police do. There'll be no keeping secrets once we're forced from this house. It's only the walls that have kept the truth hidden so long.

Nineteen

Muna showed no expression when she opened the front door and found Inspector Jordan and Mrs Hughes on the doorstep. But her heart churned with anger. Ebuka had betrayed her. When she'd brought him his mobile, he'd said his calls would be to his employer and the Housing Officer at the council, and she'd believed him. She chastised herself now for not noticing that he never addressed the people he spoke to by name.

The Inspector looked past her into the hall. 'Good afternoon, Mr Songoli. Did you intend us to come at the same time or would you rather one of us went away and came back later?'

Ebuka brought his chair to a halt. 'It was intentional,' he said. 'Mrs Hughes can substantiate what I'm about to tell you. Let the ladies in, Muna.'

I will not, Master. I don't want them here.

He moved alongside her so that she couldn't shut the door. 'You must speak in English,' he urged. 'Mrs Hughes knows you're fluent but it's impolite to let the Inspector think you don't understand what's being said.'

Muna dropped a small curtsey. 'I'm sorry, lady. Dada teaches me new words each day but I still find my own language easier. I'm glad to see you again.'

Inspector Jordan examined her curiously, and Muna experienced the same thrill of fear that she'd felt the first time she'd met her. She'd forgotten how piercing the blue eyes were – as all-seeing as Mrs Hughes's – and she shuddered to think that both whites could read what was in her mind. She stepped aside to let them in and listened solemnly while Ebuka asked her to go to the kitchen to make some tea.

'I don't think I should, Dada. You can't leave the shameful bits out of Mamma's story if you're to tell it properly. It would be better if I explained why she left.'

'I still want you to make tea, Muna.'

'There's no need,' Inspector Jordan murmured. 'I'd like to hear what your daughter has to say. You told me on the phone it was urgent, Mr Songoli.'

'It is,' he said excitedly. 'I believe my wife is dead.'

Ebuka had never learned patience. If he'd wanted to be believed, he should have told his story slowly and with guile as Muna always did. Both whites looked doubtful as they followed him into the sitting room, though perhaps it was his agitation that was worrying them. His eyes bulged alarmingly as he thrust the credit-card statement into the Inspector's hands, maintaining forcefully that if Yetunde were alive, there would be more transactions than a couple of purchases from the local supermarket.

'At the very least there should be charges from five-star hotels and department stores,' he insisted. 'She stays in the best accommodation and buys clothes and jewellery when she's angry.'

The Inspector took a seat to put herself on his level. 'You need to calm yourself and start again, Mr Songoli. At the moment I can't see why a piece of paper means your wife's dead. Do I gather she's left you?'

'I thought she had,' he said impatiently, 'but I changed my mind when I saw the statement.'

'You said she was angry. Did you have an argument?'

'A small one but it has no bearing on why she hasn't used her credit card.'

'What did your daughter mean by "shameful bits"?'

Muna sat on the sofa with her head down, a picture of timidity as she'd been on the night of Abiola's disappearance, and listened to Ebuka try to minimise his confrontation with Yetunde. Foolish man. It hadn't occurred to him that Inspector Jordan would be as interested in the reasons for Yetunde's departure as her apparent failure to use her credit card. If such a thought had crossed his mind, he would never have invited the witchy-white.

He expected Mrs Hughes to speak only of his anxiety for Yetunde – reminding her of his tears and distress – but she shook her head apologetically and told the Inspector that Mr Songoli's fight with his wife had been so violent she'd urged him to call the police.

She described Ebuka's bruises, his reluctance to re-enter the house, his relief to find it empty. She talked of the hoist being in the hall and track marks on the carpet where Mr Songoli had tried to pull himself towards his bedroom. She said she could confirm that Mrs Songoli had left because she went upstairs to check the bedrooms. She'd done the same after Olubayo's departure when Muna had come to her house, begging for help because her father was so distraught.

'Have you forgotten what you told my husband that evening?' she asked Ebuka. 'That your wife planned both exits? You were very upset about it . . . said she blamed you for Abiola's disappearance, and your relationship had suffered as a result.'

Ebuka gave his jaw a violent rub. 'That was before I knew she wasn't using her card. She can't live without it.'

The Inspector placed her finger on the page. 'She's bought four hundred pounds' worth of food.'

'Someone has,' he agreed. 'But not Yetunde.'

The words and the way he was staring at Muna had meaning for Mrs Hughes. She stirred as if preparing to speak again but Muna raised her head in order to answer first. 'There was nothing to eat after Mamma left,' she told Inspector Jordan, 'so I took the smartphone to my friend Mrs Hughes and asked her to teach me to use it. It's how Mamma always bought our food. I wanted to please Dada. He doesn't think men should be troubled with kitchen work.'

The Inspector looked enquiringly at Mrs Hughes who gave a small nod. 'How did you get your mother's card?'

'I didn't, lady. I remembered the moves she made with her finger each time she used her phone for shopping.' Muna placed her hand on the sofa and mimicked tapping a screen. 'I can't read numbers but I know the order the little boxes have to be touched, and that's all that's necessary to make the white van come. Mrs Hughes will tell you how well I can do it.'

Mrs Hughes gave another nod. 'I've never come across a child with such an agile mind. She can memorise any sequence.' She turned to Ebuka. 'It makes me wonder why you thought it right to keep her out of school, Mr Songoli. I'd hazard a guess her IQ's well above average.'

'You had no business helping her,' he retorted angrily. 'She let me think my wife was alive. When I called the credit-card company, they said the card was being used. Muna could have told me the truth then . . . but she didn't.'

The Inspector handed back the statement. 'Muna couldn't know hers were the only purchases,' she said. 'If you assumed Mrs Songoli was spending money then so would she. It's easy to be wise after the event.' She glanced at Muna. 'Why didn't you admit it this morning when the bill arrived?'

'I was afraid to, lady. I knew Dada would be angry.'

'I'm not angry,' Ebuka growled, his tone contradicting his words. 'I'm worried.' He tapped the page. 'This doesn't make sense. I know my wife.'

'Are you sure, sir? Her assault seems to have taken you by surprise. Are you going to tell me why she lost her temper? Did it have something to do with Abiola's disappearance?'

Ebuka didn't answer immediately, but when he did he echoed the excuse Muna had given Mrs Hughes. Perhaps he'd come to believe it himself. 'In a way. I wanted Muna to take me into the garden and I urged her to put on Abiola's anorak and boots because they were close at hand in the cloakroom. Yetunde became distressed when she saw her.'

'Is that all?'

'It's all I remember.'

The Inspector wasn't convinced. 'There must have been something more, sir. Violence against a person comes from pent-up rage, not momentary sadness. It's close and personal to pull a man from his chair and kick him in the head. It speaks more of long-standing resentment than distress.'

Ebuka crushed one fist inside the other. 'It makes no difference. The issue is why Yetunde isn't using her card, not why she left. How are she and my son living if they're not running up credit?'

'She has another source of income . . . a bank account you don't know about.'

Ebuka shook his head. 'Not possible. I was the only breadwinner.'

'Did you give her an allowance?'

'A little cash from time to time, otherwise she charged everything to account. I settled the bills by cheque. It's what caused the arguments after my accident. How were we going to live if I couldn't work?'

'Who wrote the cheques when you were in hospital?'

A look of weary resignation entered Ebuka's eyes. 'I signed blanks.'

'And gave them to your wife to fill in?'

'There was no other choice. It was a long journey to the rehabilitation centre and Yetunde didn't want to be away from the house for so long. She said it was because of Olubayo's epilepsy but' – his voice faltered – 'she found my condition harder to accept than I did.'

'I'm sorry,' the Inspector said with genuine sympathy. 'It was a difficult time for both of you. Abiola's loss was still raw, and it can't have helped either of you to suffer months of separation afterwards.' She leaned forward. 'You need to speak to your bank . . . find out who the cheques were made out to. If Mrs Songoli wrote them to cash, you'll have a problem, but a good private investigator may be able to trace her. It's not something the police can help you with, I'm afraid.'

Ebuka stared at the floor for several seconds. When he spoke next it was in Hausa. Did Princess keep money in the house while I was in hospital?

Muna wondered if he was trying to trick her. Had he forgotten the rows he'd had with Yetunde about writing cheques to 'cash'? She hadn't understood the meaning at the time, but she believed she did now after listening to Inspector Jordan. Was it better to pretend ignorance or knowledge?

You know she did, Master. You threw a letter from the bank at her after you came home and told her she was stupid to think turning cheques into money could hide how much she'd spent.

What did she buy with it?

Muna thought of the heavy gold chains that hung around Yetunde's sagging neck in the cellar. She had boasted to Olubayo about the clever deals she'd struck in the open-air Asian markets, refusing to listen to his warnings about Ebuka's fury when he found out. Gold was a good investment, Yetunde had said. If the case for compensation failed, she would have something of value to sell. And for once it would be the husband asking the wife for money instead of the other way round.

This time Muna decided ignorance would serve her better. I don't know, Master. I only saw her buy things with her mobile . . . the way she always did.

Ebuka pressed a thumb and finger to the bridge of his nose. The Inspector thinks she drew the money in cash and paid it into another bank. Do you understand what that means?

Not really, Master.

It means she may have a card I don't know about. Did you ever notice her tap a different number into the screen?

Muna was tempted to say yes. He would surely believe then that Princess had stolen his money in order to leave him. But she saw how intently he was watching her. The witchy-white had praised her cleverness too well. He would ask Muna next to show him the order Yetunde's fingers had touched the squares.

No, Master. If I had, I'd have remembered it.

Disappointment made him irritable. He smacked his palms against his legs and spoke in English. 'You see and hear everything that happens in this house,' he cried angrily. 'How can you be ignorant of Yetunde stealing from me?'

Perhaps Ebuka was right to distrust women. Neither white took kindly to him raising his voice to Muna. Mrs Hughes leaned forward to protect her while Inspector Jordan warned Ebuka she would have to take action if she had cause to believe he was visiting his frustration against his wife on his daughter. In legislation here, the welfare of the child took priority.

She turned to Muna. 'Do you understand what that means, Muna?'

'I think so, lady. I think you're saying that Dada isn't allowed to hurt me.'

'Does he?'

Muna smiled into her knowing blue eyes. 'Of course not, lady. Dada loves me very much. If he was unkind to me, I would have told my friend Mrs Hughes. She has asked me many times if there are things she can do to help me.'

Muna couldn't tell if it was her words or Ebuka's sudden rush of tears that persuaded the Inspector and Mrs Hughes to leave. Both women looked uncomfortable as he lowered his head to his hands and sobbed uncontrollably. In the hall, they advised Muna to call his doctor, expressing concern for his depressed and troubled state of mind.

She asked timidly how medicine could help pay the rent since his greatest anxiety was about losing the house. 'When everything's gone and strangers are living here, Mamma and Olubayo won't be able to find us,' she explained. 'That's what's making Dada sad. He doesn't know what to do or who to ask for help. It shames and frightens him to have no money.'

The Inspector looked thoughtful. 'That would certainly explain why he's upset with your mother. Did she know she was putting the house at risk?'

Muna shook her head, recalling words she'd said to Mrs Hughes. 'Mamma doesn't think when she's angry, lady. Her only desire is to show Dada how distressed she is.'

'But what caused this anger? Your father never really explained.'

'Everything, lady. Olubayo's epilepsy . . . Dada's accident . . . but mostly Abiola's loss.' Muna tried a phrase she'd learned from the television talk shows she now watched every afternoon: 'Dada wanted her to stop blaming herself and move on, but that just made her think he didn't care about Abiola as much as she did.'

'And she resented him for it?'

'I'm not sure, lady. I don't know what "resented" means.'

'Disliked him . . . held a grudge . . . believed he wasn't interested in how she felt.'

Mrs Hughes shook her head. 'I imagine her greatest resentment is directed against the police,' she murmured. 'Abiola was abducted off our streets, yet the family's had no justice . . . no funeral . . . no closure. I'm not surprised Mrs Songoli's emotions are in turmoil. Her husband's also.'

A faint flush stained the Inspector's cheeks. 'Tell your father I'll put in a request for the rent to be paid,' she told Muna gruffly, turning the handle of the front door. 'It's in no one's interests to have you evicted while your brother's case remains open.'

Muna ducked her head in gratitude, and received a reluctant smile in return. It never ceased to amaze her how easily whites were embarrassed into doing what she wanted. She watched from inside the hall as the women walked away, and from the bowels of the cellar she heard the Devil laugh. The sound was tiny – a breath fluttering through the floor – but she felt its tremors run joyously through her body.

SPRING

Twenty

Muna squatted in the dust of the chamber and touched her finger to Yetunde's left cheek. She hadn't visited since joining Olubayo to his family, and she felt a terrible disappointment to find Yetunde so shrunken and shrivelled. For a time, after Muna had peeled the parcel tape from her mouth, Yetunde had been pleasing to look at, but now her lips were drawn back from her teeth in an ugly grimace and her lids lay flat across her sockets as if her eyes had retracted inside her head.

So much of her flesh had withered that the rings on her fingers and the chains about her neck seemed out of proportion; as did the blue silk kaba that hung in bulky folds where the bulbous breasts and monstrous stomach had dried to nothing. It was hard to recognise Yetunde in this little grey corpse.

Abiola and Olubayo were the same. They lay in the dust – Abiola curled on his side and Olubayo flat on his back – with hollowed eyes and teeth protruding from their mouths. Muna doubted even Ebuka would find a likeness to his sons in their emaciated faces and taut, unfriendly sneers. She regretted the sense of revulsion she felt. Her pleasure at being able to love and caress them had been very brief.

She tried to lift Yetunde's hand but the desiccated skin was set hard, holding the woman rigid. Princess would sit for ever with her head tilted back against the cellar wall unless Muna removed her. Such an idea had seemed impossible when Ebuka had first mentioned leaving, but Muna had learned from Mrs Hughes how easy it was to transport the contents of one house to another.

Ebuka would organise a lorry, and Muna would pack loose items into boxes and trunks before sealing them with parcel tape to prevent the contents spilling out. Since only she would know what was inside, she must mark the outsides with something that told the carriers where to leave the boxes at the other end. Mrs Hughes knew from experience how tedious and tiring it was to find kitchen crockery in upstairs rooms.

This knowledge had dissipated Muna's fears of moving, a subject that had been mentioned frequently since counsellors, occupational therapists and social workers began to take an interest in her and Ebuka. All were agreed that a house with three storeys, a gravel drive and inadequate bathing facilities downstairs was unsuitable for a man in a wheelchair. It seemed it wasn't possible to have the rent paid without accepting help and advice on everything else.

Most of the advice was beneficial to Ebuka. Once his right to receive assistance was confirmed, there was talk of supplying him with a modified car, offers of training to re-enter the workplace and intercession with his employer to keep his job open for another six months. More importantly, constant visitors – often unscheduled – meant Muna could no longer punish him through neglect.

She regretted this less than she thought she would since the most regular visitor was for her: a handsome young black man who came every afternoon to teach her reading, writing and arithmetic. Muna never tired of learning with him. He taught her in English and her heart fluttered joyfully each time he praised her quickness of understanding.

Ebuka wouldn't allow them to be alone. He attended every lesson, frowning ferociously when the tutor's approval elicited a smile. Muna could have told Ebuka it was the praise she liked and not the person – she had no feelings for people – but his irritation persuaded her to smile more. Jealousy, however misguided, was as good a punishment as neglect.

There was no predicting Ebuka's emotions. Some days he paid Muna as little notice as when she'd been a slave; other days when she wore dresses that Yetunde had bought for herself when she was younger and slimmer – stored in the trunks in the cellar – his hot eyes never left her. He was at his most irritable on the occasions when Mrs Hughes complimented Muna on how pretty she was becoming and told her it wouldn't be long before she had boyfriends.

Each time, he warned the girl strongly to forget any ideas of marriage. She was an illegal immigrant in a foreign land and could do nothing without papers. But Muna's new ability to read allowed her to search for the documents that Yetunde had used to steal her from the orphanage and bring her to England, and these included a birth certificate and a passport in the name of Muna Songoli, and a second birth certificate, faded and torn, in the name of Muna Lawal.

She showed them to Ebuka and asked why he'd lied to her. When he didn't answer, she set fire to everything relating to Muna Lawal, saying she didn't choose to have an unknown man for a father or a prostitute for a mother. Her life would be better now that she could prove she was Ebuka Songoli's daughter and had the same rights as he had.

His eyes filled with tears and she asked him why. Was his life not improved by her burning the evidence that a slave had lived in his house? Ebuka should be pleased. He need never fear discovery again. How often had he wished Muna gone in order to bring an end to her punishments?

But he wept and said his heart would break if she left him. He was more attached to his little slave than he'd ever been to his family, and longed for her company even when she treated him harshly. She'd been right to tell Inspector Jordan that he loved her. No other face pleased him so deeply. He couldn't bear to lose her, and wished he'd destroyed all the papers so that her only choice was to stay.

Muna watched without emotion as the tears spilled down his cheeks. Unable to feel love or affection herself, she thought Ebuka weak and foolish to say such things. Could he not see how powerful little Muna would become if all she had to do was threaten to leave? She would never put such a threat into action. Ebuka had no understanding of her if he imagined she could live with another man. Even the thought of being touched by her handsome young tutor made her sick.

The cellar felt cold suddenly and Muna drew her dressing gown more tightly about her as she leaned forward to stare into Yetunde's sightless eyes. There was no joy to be had from this mummified body. Dead, Yetunde could never acknowledge Muna as her mistress, or feel anger that a piccaninny had taken possession of everything she'd once owned. Perhaps it was a form of love to hate a person so much that life seemed empty without them.

She took a pair of secateurs from her pocket and trapped Yetunde's thumb between the blades.

The mind is a mysterious thing, Princess, she said. However hard I try, I can't stop thinking about you. It may have something to do with forgiveness, which the counsellor says brings closure. I'm not sure what that means except the Master hasn't thought about you at all since he forgave you for stealing his money. Perhaps I'd feel differently if you were alive and you could tell me you were sorry for taking me . . . but I don't think so. I'd know you were lying. It pleased you too much to possess a life that didn't belong to you.

She squeezed the blades, smiling when they crunched together. She'd watched the gardener use secateurs to snip dead wood from shrubs and it seemed parched skin and brittle bone were as easily severed. Poor Princess. Her thumb popped from her hand like a discarded twig, making a faint clink as it hit the stone floor. Dried of blood and moisture, it was as light as a feather and Muna examined it curiously before placing it carefully on Yetunde's lap.

She turned to nudge Abiola's knee and marvelled as the body shifted easily in the dust. There was no weight in any of them. Even Olubayo, the last to die, moved at her touch. Next time she would bring a saw in order to dismember her trophies as efficiently as the gardener had hewn dead limbs from trees. And when the day came to place the parts into the trunks and suitcases on the other side of the wall, she would cover them with duvets and pillows and ask Mrs Hughes to make a mark which said they must be left in Muna's bedroom. Ebuka would never think to search for pillows, and Muna would keep the secret for ever that his wife and sons lay buried in linen beneath her bed.

She stroked Yetunde's cheek again. There will be no tears for you and your sons, Princess. No one will find you. You are mine to do with as I like.

Her words echoed off the chamber walls – *you are mine . . . you are mine* – and she shivered violently as the cold became so intense that her breath, warmer than the air, drifted like smoke across Yetunde's face. Muna felt the metal of the secateurs burn like ice against her fingers and dropped them into her pocket before staring into the darkness beyond the chamber door.

The fabric of the kaba lifted on Yetunde's chest, and for a shocked moment Muna thought the corpse had taken a breath. Her heart thumped painfully until the air warmed and the scent of jasmine filled her nostrils, reminding her of the schoolyard where she'd been happy.

She put her mouth to Yetunde's ear. The Devil is here, Princess, but not to give you justice. It's Muna He protects. He was in this place when you brought me to it and He gave me strength. You were foolish to take a child you knew nothing about. I was never so abandoned and unloved that you could steal me without fear of being punished.

Muna paused on the cellar steps when the light from her torch showed her that the door at the top was ajar, and she chided herself for not guessing where the breeze was coming from. The hall beyond was in darkness but she had little hope the latch had come undone of its own accord. As she raised the beam to the aperture, the gap widened, revealing Ebuka, hunched in pyjamas, in his wheelchair. He lifted a hand to shield his eyes from the brightness then leaned inside the doorjamb to flick on the cellar light.

The rod was across his knees and his mobile was clasped in his right fist. When he saw Muna, he gestured to her to keep coming towards him. I thought you were a burglar, he growled, moving his chair backwards to let her out. It's the middle of the night. What on earth are you doing?

Muna pushed the torch into her dressing-gown pocket to mask the shape of the secateurs. I come here often, Master, she answered calmly. Sometimes I find it easier to sleep on a hard stone floor than I do in a bed. It was my home for many years and not all memories of it are bad.

I heard you speaking to someone.

Only to myself, Master. I learned to do it when I lived down here. A voice was comforting when the darkness made me lonely and afraid. I used to practise words each night after Princess forbade me from talking.

She made to move past Ebuka, but he barred her way with the rod. Something scraped across the floor, he said. It sounded like a door closing.

Do you not remember what the cellar looks like, Master? You came often enough. There's no door . . . only walls and a floor.

Then what was the noise I heard? And why did you sweep the stones afterwards? I didn't imagine these things.

Muna pointed to her bare feet. I have no shoes, Master. Princess's feet were so big that none of hers fit me. I pulled a trunk into the middle of the floor to see if there were any inside from when Abiola was a small boy but all I found were slippers. I tried walking in them but they fell off if I didn't slide them along the floor. Mrs Hughes says we should give such things to charity. It's what white people do with clothes they don't need any more.

Ebuka was only half-convinced. He eased her aside to look down the cellar steps. I was sure someone was with you.

Would you like to see for yourself, Master? If I fetch the hoist to lower you from your chair, I could help you down the same way Mr Hughes did. I'm stronger than I used to be.

Ebuka returned the rod to his lap with a grunt of amusement. And then what? You abandon me at the bottom? I wouldn't trust you not to lock me in all night if it suited you. I'm sure you'd think it a worthy punishment.

Muna felt the first tiny tremors of the Devil's laughter rise through the floorboards. I would, Master . . . but at least you'd know for certain there's no one hiding there. If a person breathed, you would hear him.

Ebuka shivered. It's cold. Turn off the light and close the door. We'll order some shoes in the morning . . . dresses too if you like.

Muna touched the switch and plunged them into darkness again. She heard Ebuka grumble that he couldn't see anything, and Muna thought how vulnerable he'd made himself. With a single push, she could pitch him down the steps and his life would be ended for ever. The Devil was tempting her to do it. His laughter swelled and grew, creating such strong vibrations that Muna fancied she saw the walls of the cellar begin to crack.

For once, she was fearful of so much power. She wasn't ready to lose Ebuka yet. Not while she still had need of him. With sudden decision she pulled the door to and stood with her forehead pressed against the wood, listening to the laughter fade. When the floor stopped trembling and there was only silence, she felt for the switch at the bottom of the stairs and flooded the hall with brilliant light.

You must be careful when you open this door, Master, she warned sternly, turning to look at him. If you misjudge your distance or lean too far inside, your chair will tip forward and you'll fall again.

With a wry smile, Ebuka manoeuvred himself backwards. You seemed to like the idea a moment ago. Are you developing a sense of humor at last?

A frown of genuine puzzlement creased the girl's brow. Why would I want you to die, Master? I enjoy being your daughter.

He was surprised by the strength of feeling in her tone. My mistake. I could have sworn it was the idea of giving me a push that was making you laugh.

Muna shook her head. I wasn't laughing, Master.

Ebuka studied her curiously for a moment then turned his chair towards the dining-room. It was a happy sound, he said over his shoulder. You should do it more often. But next time let it out through your mouth instead of holding it in for fear of being heard. There hasn't been enough laughter in this house.

MR & MRS R.G.F. HUGHES
25 FORTIS ROW
LONDON N10

Dear Inspector Jordan,

Even as I write this letter, I don't know if I'll send it.
Several times I've reached for the telephone, only to
change my mind about calling. If I had facts to support
my suspicions, I'd feel more confident about talking to
you. But I don't. My concerns for Muna Songoli are
based entirely on a retired teacher's intuition.

For six years I had no idea she existed. I used to see
a face at the windows occasionally but it wasn't until the
newspapers said Abiola had a sister that I realised who the
face belonged to. Mrs Songoli was an extremely intimidat-
ing woman. On the one occasion I visited, she made it clear
I wasn't welcome. I didn't try again. My only contact with
the family was to nod to Ebuka or his sons if I passed them
in the street. They were polite but unfriendly.

When I finally met and spoke with Muna, every
instinct told me something was wrong. She was clearly
malnourished, showed signs of abuse, and her looks were
so different from the other Songolis that I found it hard
to believe she was Ebuka and Yetunde's child.

I wish I'd spoken out at the time but my husband persuaded me you'd have uncovered anything untoward during your investigation into Abiola's disappearance. Also Muna was extremely convincing when she spoke of Yetunde and Ebuka as her parents. She had several opportunities to talk to me in private, most notably when she came to my house, but she always referred to them as Mamma and Dada.

She has never deviated from that line, yet, from my experience, the bond between her and Ebuka isn't typical of a father-daughter relationship. Ebuka's disability means he's completely reliant on her, and he becomes noticeably agitated at any suggestion she might leave to forge a life of her own. His love for her is very strong. I would go so far as to say passionate. He's certainly possessive of her time and attention.

Throughout my acquaintance with Muna, I've been astonished by the alertness of her mind and her quite exceptional memory. She understands and remembers everything. However, she persists in the story that her thinness—less pronounced since her mother left—and her previous unwillingness to leave the house, were due to brain damage. When I challenge her on it, pointing out how quickly she learnt to read and write, she tells me she must have got 'better'.

Since I can't accept that, I've searched for a different reason why a young girl might remain closeted inside a house for six years. The only one that makes sense to me is that Muna was brought to England as a slave and 'adopted' as a 'daughter' when tragedy engulfed the family and police entered the house.

I appreciate that slavery is a strong allegation to make but I've had sleepless nights worrying about Muna. She was a frightened, near-inarticulate, half-starved child when I first encountered her, and she's only begun to develop physically and mentally since she came into contact with the outside world after Mrs Songoli's departure.

She remains adamant that Ebuka is her father but I struggle to believe it. In my opinion, she's been so thoroughly brainwashed and abused (physically, sexually and verbally) that she clings to the devil she knows rather than put her trust in people she's been taught to fear.

If you're reading this letter, it means I've ignored my husband's warnings. His view, strongly expressed, is that Muna will regress if she's taken into care and forced to testify about things she doesn't want known. He urges me to let her decide for herself how and when she wants justice.

Yours sincerely,

The dust settles.
The air warms.
Spiders spin their webs.
No one is there.

Darkness hides.
Darkness deceives.
Darkness is within.
Waiting.